THE RELUCTANT BLADE

The Reluctant Blade

GERRIT VAN ECK

First Printing, 2025

Acknowledgements

This book came about through the contributions of many people, and without their help I wouldn't be sitting here struggling to figure out what to write for this section. I wish I could do more to thank you all than scribble a little note on the part of the book that everyone skips, but this will have to do for now.

First and foremost, shout out to my fantastic friends over at CC. You guys all helped in different ways, each of them invaluable. Whether it be beta reading, giving me feedback on my worldbuilding, or answering my questions about the same scenes over and over until I finally nailed it down, I can't imagine how this book could have happened without your guys' support. Thank you for making this a possibility, you're all incredible.

To my editor, Amanda Clarke, thank you for taking my manuscript and improving it in more ways than I can count. You were a delight to work with in every sense of the word, and I'm glad I was able to find such a great editor. This book would have been a much worse read if not for your careful eyes.

Most importantly, shout out to my wife, Sara. Your endless support and unwavering confidence in my ability to finish this project are the main reasons it happened. You never doubted me, even when I definitely doubted myself. Thank you for always having my back, I couldn't have done this without you.

Chapter 1

Serennia winced with every dab of the alcohol-soaked rag against her cheek. Each gentle touch sent a brief lance of pain through the side of her face, and she wondered if it was really as necessary as Laerine had insisted.

"Hold still. The more you move about, the longer this is going to take." Laerine was a matronly woman, and she spoke with a level of patience that most could only aspire to. The woman had been the second-in-command for most of her life at Rosewine Estate, through three separate Lords. Her greying hair was pulled back into a bun, revealing a face that somehow managed to be both wrinkled and vibrant.

Serennia sat with her in the manor's infirmary, which was little more than a spare room they had filled with various medical supplies. She looked around at the various tinctures and ointments that lined the shelves, filling the air with an alcoholic stench that pervaded through every inch of the confined space.

"I can't help it." The cloth touched her cut again, and it was all she could do to keep from jerking her head away. "Are you almost done?"

"You know, the more you ask that, the more time I have to spend answering and the less time I spend getting it done." A few more wipes and Laerine at last set the rag down on a nearby table. She held Serennia's chin in one hand to give her a final inspection, then clicked her tongue as she stood from her seat.

"Thankfully, it's not too deep, but I'm going to put some salve on it to speed the healing anyway." Laerine retrieved a jar of pale jelly from a drawer, unscrewing the lid with a small amount of effort. She scooped a small dab onto her finger and smeared it across the cut on Serennia's face. It was cold and soothing, a refreshing change from the sting of the antiseptic.

Serennia rose to her feet and touched a hand to the wound. Her fingers came away sticky, the sweet, floral scent lingering from the brief contact. She grimaced. That would take time to get used to, or she'd scratch an itch and find her fingernails caked with half-dried salve.

"You go along and find yourself some dinner. I'll clean up here and find you downstairs." Before Serennia could respond, Laerine had turned and was busy tidying up.

Serennia stepped into the hallway, rows of doors lining either side. The last of the day's light streamed in through the windows, casting long shadows along the carpeted floor. It was a short walk to the kitchen, the scent hitting her before the room was within sight.

Inside the kitchen, a team of cooks was busy putting the final touches on the night's meal, hustling to and fro from one side to the other. Among them was Cal, whose bright yellow jacket denoted him as a trained noble-chef. A lifetime of working with food had rounded out his figure, his hands calloused from years of wielding a knife. The man looked like he'd be more at home in a galley than a manor. Serennia was unsure whether his baldness was by choice or simply a product of aging. Any time she'd asked as a child, he would answer with some offhand remark about how he "can't get any hair in the food if he doesn't have any."

Upon her entrance, Cal stopped stirring his soup (or maybe it was a sauce of some kind, she couldn't tell) and greeted her with a cheery wave. "Look who finally decided to come 'round! I was starting to think the smell of my cooking turned you away!" He was a boisterous man, hardly ever speaking below an excited shout.

Serennia smiled and let out a brief chuckle. "Better late than never, though, right?"

Cal was about to respond when his eyes froze on her cheek. She had considered trying to hide the injury from him, but anything she could have done would have only drawn more attention.

"What happened there?" Cal asked, one finger pointing to the red line that traced her cheekbone. "I swear on the Five, Ren, if he did this to you, I'll make him pay for it."

"It's nothing, Cal, I swear." Serennia tried to turn her face away from his scrutiny, but he turned her face the other way with a finger. He leaned forward until his face was level with hers, samples of the night's dinner wafting across on his breath. She could feel his gaze piercing through her, like the wound had given him an opening into her soul.

"He can't keep getting away with this. He can't keep treating you like his own personal punching bag any time he gets mad." Cal grabbed the hand towel off his shoulder and wrung it like a neck.

"I just don't understand why he hates me so much," Serennia said, careful to keep the emotion from her voice. "What did I ever do to him?"

"You've done absolutely nothing. You're a wonderful young woman with a full life ahead of you. Crennel Brathis is just a pathetic worm with a superiority complex."

"Why can't he just be nice like Lord Hauber?" Her voice wavered, and she resisted the tears with every ounce of energy she had. She wasn't a child anymore. She was only a couple of years away from adulthood, even if Crennel refused to treat her as anything more than a snivelling child.

"Because people like him need to feel powerful. Deep down he knows he's nothing but a weak shell of a man. It ain't nothing against you; you just happen to be the only one he thinks he can get away with treating that way."

Serennia took in a deep breath, burying her sadness beneath years of practised bravery. "I'll never understand how someone like him could come from the same family as Lord Hauber."

Hauber Brathis had been the Lord of Rosewine Estate for decades and had taken Serennia in when he'd found her wandering the streets. He'd treated her like his own daughter, even introducing her as such at social gatherings. When a sudden illness claimed his life a few years back, his nephew, Crennel, had succeeded him. The years since had been a nightmare that grew steadily worse as time wore on.

"Lord Hauber was one of a kind. We would be lucky to see another man like him in our lifetime." Cal returned the towel to its spot over his shoulder, then cut a small piece off the end of the roast and passed it to Serennia.

The meat fell apart in her mouth, the seasonings spreading across her palette with each bite. She tried to savour it as long as she could, though there was only so much she could do with such a small morsel. When she was finished, she let out a satisfied exhale.

"Thank you, Cal. Amazing as always."

"Glad you like it. Now you better get going. I don't want Crennel to catch you back here if he decides he has a problem with tonight's meal. If he does, I can't promise I won't knock him halfway to the moon, and that would cause more problems than it solves."

Serennia gave a resigned sigh, though she knew he was right. She gave him a quick hug, her arms tight around his torso. Cal responded with a gentle pat on the back of her head.

"I wish there was more I could do to help you, Ren. For now, you'll just have to keep your chin up and hope that the sun will break the clouds."

Serennia cloaked her pain with a shallow smile. Cal had given her that advice countless times in the past, yet with every passing day it felt less and less like she would ever see the sun again. Each morning she woke up feeling emptier, each smile more forced and hollow.

As much as she didn't want to be on her own, she knew the dangers of anyone other than the cooks being in the kitchen. Crennel was terrified of being poisoned, and she didn't need to risk his ire any more than she already had. She said a final goodbye to Cal, then left to haunt the halls—her only hope that she could make it the rest of the night without crossing Crennel's path.

The hallways were lavish, like everything else at Rosewine. Plush carpet ran down the centre, dotted with small tables that bore vases of flowers or small artworks. This late at night the only illumination came from the ensconced glowstones along the wall just above her head. Imbued with magic and forged only in the Arcanaeum, the glowstones alone were a symbol of wealth.

After a few minutes of wandering, Serennia stopped to lean against a windowsill and look out at the town before her. She yearned for the freedom of the city, but Crennel had forbidden her from leaving the estate almost as soon as he'd taken over. Lights shone like stars in the distance, candles flickering in windows and doorways, illuminating the busy streets of Alcress. Even this late in the evening, hardly a single street was empty. People hurried from work or dinner or strolled to one of the hubs of nightlife that dotted the town.

On the few occasions Serennia had been able to leave the estate without supervision, she had enjoyed visiting the merchants. She had never been able to buy anything—having no money of her own—but she enjoyed perusing their wares all the same. The shop owners always seemed to enjoy the company of someone truly interested in their goods and were always eager to show off their newest pieces.

Looking out at the city, Serennia felt like a caged bird, her head filled with dreams of soaring. Crennel had clipped her wings years ago, scared that she might fly away and let the world know how truly awful he was. She pressed her face so close to the glass that she could see the reflection of her pale irises, wishing she could somehow melt through the window.

The red line across her cheek stood in stark contrast to the tawny brown of her skin, which was almost unnoticeable in her reflection compared to the pure white hair that framed it. When she was a child, she'd often been made fun of for her features; children would joke that she was an old lady, her hair having already lost its colour. Had they never seen a Garleshi person before?

Her eyes dropped to the courtyard outside the estate. She had spent so many evenings there with Lord Hauber, practising her secret talent away from watchful eyes. He had insisted that she know how to use it, despite always telling her she was never to do so outside the courtyard. What was the point of having a gift if she had to keep it hidden from the world?

One hand went to her pocket where she kept the pendant he had gotten her on their first trip to the market together. It was a simple piece: a small ruby wrapped in thin, wiry iron that hung from a cord. She hadn't worn the thing in years; it had grown too tight to be worn comfortably, and she thought it looked a touch childish. But it hadn't left her pocket since the day she'd stopped wearing it.

Footsteps sounded in the distance, growing louder with each passing second. The guards were running towards her, evident from the clattering of armour that echoed down the halls. *Did someone break into the manor or something? Why are the guards so fired up all of a sudden?*

"There she is!" One of them turned the corner and locked eyes with Serennia. "Seize her!" He pointed at her, and she felt fear spike through her body. She'd never seen the guards so worked up before.

She ran. The guards sprinted after her, closing the distance at a steady pace. They were trained for this sort of exertion, while she was relying solely on the burst of energy coursing through her. She turned the corner and stumbled over her feet, falling to the floor in a mess. Serennia rolled over onto her back in time to see the guards standing over her, their spears levelled at her chest.

"You think you can try to assassinate Lord Brathis and get away with it?" The guard captain sneered at her, the point of his spear only inches from her throat. A polished helmet covered his entire head, his vicious scowl and angry eyes all that was visible. "You're going to regret being so bold, brat."

"Assassinate? What?" *Someone had tried to kill Crennel?* As much as she hated him, Serennia would never do something like that. "I didn't do anything, I swear!"

"Don't play dumb with me. Someone poisoned his food, and several of the cooks said they saw you in the kitchen while they were preparing. They said you distracted Cal and slipped something in."

"I didn't! I swear to you!"

"Say whatever you want, it's not going to change any minds. We've got orders to kill you on sight. Seems Lord Brathis has finally come to his senses. He should've been rid of you a long time ago."

Serennia longed for the old guards, the nice men who would sometimes play cards with her out on the terrace. There had only been a few of them then, just enough to watch the main gate and patrol the perimeter on rotation. Crennel had fired all of them within months of taking over and had replaced them with an ever-growing number of men who seemed more like bloodthirsty mercenaries than estate guards.

The captain took a step towards her, his spear pulled back, preparing to thrust. "No, stop!" Serennia closed her eyes and held her hands out.

She felt a tingle flow through her arms to her fingertips, followed by a sound like someone choking on water drunk too fast. Before she opened her eyes, she knew what had happened. She'd had no choice. It was either them or her.

When she worked up the courage to open her eyes, all the guards were splayed out across the ground, gripping various injuries across their bodies. The captain's throat had been pierced clean through the centre, pouring blood onto the ground around him. Two of the guards looked like they had died instantly, though Serennia wasn't sure if that was better or worse. At least the others had a chance, if they were lucky.

Serennia pulled her hands to her mouth as she fought the urge to vomit. She hadn't meant to kill them. She had just wanted to live, hoping to injure them, maybe slow them down. Not this.

Her feet were unsteady beneath her as she struggled to process the grisly sight before her. One guard reached out and grabbed her foot, forcing a scream from her lungs that echoed down the hallway that now seemed too dark. The dying guard locked eyes with her, and she watched as the life faded from them. His grip loosened slowly until he no longer had the strength to hold on; his hand fell limp to the floor. Serennia's whole body trembled.

She found herself running down the hallway. When had she decided to do that? Her brain felt foggy and distant, her body acting on instinct. All she wanted was to get out. Out of the hallway, out of the estate, out of the city. Just a couple more minutes and she would reach the front door. Then she could be free, away from everything.

A figure lurched out from around the corner and grabbed her by the throat, the sudden arrest of momentum causing a crushing pain in her neck. Crennel pressed her against the wall, his face somehow weaker looking than usual. Vomit clung to the corners of his mouth, the putrid stench mingling with his booze-riddled breath, the perfect compliment to his wild eyes and frantic blond hair. Even in his weakened state, he was strong enough to keep hold of her. She struggled against him without success.

"I should have killed you the moment I took this estate, you bitch." His voice was raspy and strained, though no less angry than usual. He held a knife in his free hand, the polished steel glinting in the soft light of the hallway. "I'm going to make sure you die slowly, and I am going to enjoy it."

For the first time in years, Serennia was afraid of the wicked sneer that spread across his face. "No. Please. It wasn't me. I promise." It was hard to speak with Crennel crushing her windpipe. Each word was a fight, forced out with what little breath she could manage.

"Too late." The knife pressed against her stomach until a thin line of blood trickled out, finding a path down the blade.

"Stop..." Serennia barely got the word out. The edges of her vision were blurring, her eyes losing the ability to focus. She didn't want to hurt anyone else. But she didn't have a choice.

Her arm dropped, half falling and half swiping at Crennel's hand. As it fell, a thin, opalescent blade materialized before her fingers. It sliced clean across Crennel's wrist, his knife dropping to the floor as his hand jerked open in pain. His other hand released its grip on her throat, grasping the fresh cut. Serennia dropped to her knees on the floor.

Crennel's eyes were wide, a layer of shock merging with the anguish that flooded them. Magic without an arcane focus was supposed to be impossible, and even *with* a focus of some kind, it was supposed to take years of study to accomplish in any sort of meaningful way. If anyone knew it was something she was capable of, it could be the end of her.

Judging by the look on Crennel's face, Lord Hauber had taken her secret to his grave.

Serennia drove her fist between Crennel's legs as hard as she could, desperate to cause him pain. The wiry man doubled over, blood seeping from between his fingers. As she watched him struggle, she realized she had an opportunity. She could finish him, right here and now, and never have to worry about him again. She could put an end to the nightmare that had plagued her for years.

But she wasn't a murderer. *I killed those guards.* That had been different. That had been survival.

Serennia ran, dashing towards the front doors of the estate. She had to get out before Crennel sent more of his soldiers after her. There were enough of them on the property to overwhelm her, magic or not. Her only hope was to put as much distance between her and them as possible.

When she reached the foyer, Laerine stood in front of the main doors. The woman looked at Serennia with a sad, resigned smile. Without a word, she stepped aside and pushed open the heavy, oaken doors that led to the front gardens. Serennia paused while she searched for the right words to say. Her mouth opened for a fraction of a second before Laerine silenced her with a hand and a shake of the head. Serennia gave her a nod and the quickest hug she could manage, then pushed off and continued her panicked escape.

She burst out into the courtyard, the colourful gardens and well-trimmed hedges sprawled out before her. The cold night air sent a jolt through her body as she drew in heavy breaths, desperate to get air back into her lungs. Her threadbare shirt and trousers did little to block the chill in the breeze.

Her feet couldn't carry her fast enough. She scrambled over the wrought iron that ran around the perimeter of the garden, careful not to cut herself on the metal rosebuds that adorned the top, and landed on her feet with a soft *thud*. She looked frantically in all directions; it appeared that all the guards on duty had been summoned to the house to deal with her. Crennel's overzealousness to kill her had saved her life.

She couldn't hide in Alcress. The city was sizable, but the handful of nobles in the area owned everything. No matter where she went, word would make its way back to Crennel. Her only hope was to leave town.

Her knees burned and her feet ached as she continued to run through the criss-crossing streets, drawing a variety of glances from passersby. In the distance, she could see a horse-drawn wagon headed towards the city gates.

The wagon's meandering pace made it easy for Serennia to close the distance, and within minutes she was right behind it, though she slowed to a walk in hopes of not drawing too much more attention. The walking hurt more than the running.

Freshly harvested grain was piled up under a tarp, strapped down in the corners against the wind. When she was positive that nobody was looking, it was easy enough for her to slither beneath the canvas and find a place to hide among the wheat—in case one of the city authorities inspected the cargo before its departure.

Peeking out of the small gap between the tarp and the wooden sides, she watched as buildings shrank before her. It was painful, knowing she would be leaving the place that had been her home for so long. Maybe one day she would return, so she could thank Cal and Laerine properly for all the kindness they had shown her.

In the meantime, she listened to the wagon wheels clatter against the cobblestones, feeling the cart jostle beneath her, and watched as the city moved away. Living in Alcress had always felt like an unending expansion of brick and road. As it faded into the distance, it seemed almost embarrassingly small.

Chapter 2

A few hours had passed since Serennia had left Alcress when the chill began to sink into her bones. She hadn't felt a cold so invasive since the days after the raid on her parents' house, when she'd been forced to spend weeks hiding in the wilderness. It was the kind of cold that gripped you from the inside until your blood felt like it would turn to ice. Each shiver brought back memories from that night, memories she tried to fight and rebury, though she'd have had as much luck trying to warm herself with a candle.

She felt a pressure building in her nose and whispered a curse to herself. Was the wind whipping fast enough to cover the sound? If the buffeting of the tarp was any indication, she had a chance, however slim it might be. The sneeze ripped itself from her lungs, muffled by her hands clasped over her face. She waited with bated breath to see if the driver noticed. When the wagon continued to move, she let out a relieved exhale. An instant later another sneeze shot through her, so sudden she didn't have time to bring her hands up.

The wagon rolled to a stop. She heard the driver drop to the ground beside the horse, followed by footsteps that circled to the back of the cart. His voice came next, tinged with a warning. "I know you're there. Show yourself."

Serennia didn't move. Her options were limited, and none of them were enticing. She hoped that if she remained silent, he would think it had been a trick of the wind or some unseen animal.

"I don't want to lift this tarp up and expose my goods to the elements, but I will if you don't come out willingly. And if anything gets damaged, it'll be your hide that pays for it."

With a deep, resigned sigh, Serennia crawled her way around the haystack to the back of the wagon. As she emerged from underneath the tarp, the first thing she saw was the sharp bolt of a crossbow, aimed right between her eyes. Iron determination was etched onto the man's face, his eyes hardened and steady. It was clear he'd dealt with problems like her before and had no reservations about doing so again.

"Who are you, and why are you stowing away in my cart?"

Serennia stared down the length of the weapon and knew she had no option but the truth. "I needed to get away from Alcress, and this was the only way I could."

He gave her an appraising look, and she tried to give him one back. "Why're you in such a hurry to leave town? You some kind of criminal?"

"No, I promise I'm not. I'm just...running away from home." She hated how weak those words made her sound. They did no justice to everything she'd suffered in the years since Lord Hauber's death. A part of her wanted to explain everything to the man, to put all of Crennel's sins out in the open, but she could tell it wouldn't do any good.

"Even if that's true, I can't bring you any further. If the guards in Ruddreth inspect my cargo and find you they'll think I'm some kind of smuggler." His weapon lowered so that it pointed at the wagon rather than her face.

"You can drop me off outside the city. They'll never know. Please." Serennia hated to beg, but the storm was getting worse, and she'd never reach the city on her own before the elements did her in. She'd done more than her fair share of surviving in the wilderness and had barely made it out alive. She doubted she'd be so lucky again.

The man considered her plea for the barest fraction of a second. "Sorry, kid. This is the end of your ride." He gestured to the side with his head. Serennia hopped down and stood in front of him, her eyes boring into his, willing him to change his mind. His face seemed to portray a hint of regret, though he didn't say anything.

Serennia trudged away, anger making her footsteps heavier than they needed to be. The rain had already soaked through her clothes, and it took a conscious effort not to shiver. She refused to let that damn man see any sign of weakness. He watched her walk away, likely to ensure she didn't try anything while his back was turned. It wasn't until she had put a great distance between them that she heard the clatter of wheels rolling away.

* * * * *

The storm raged on with the fury of a jaded god, the cold wind and harsh rains attacking from every angle so that every minute felt like an hour. Serennia had no idea how long she had been walking. That was the problem with nighttime. During the day, the sun made it clear how much more time you had together. The moon was much less helpful.

She should have known better than to assume anything would go right for her. She was alone, stranded along the highway. Even the sky was punishing her. The wind bit through her meagre clothing; the rain had long since rendered it useless. She kept her hands tucked under her armpits, though the cold didn't seem to care. The gales whipped so loudly she could barely hear her teeth as they chattered against each other.

When her feet felt like they were about to rebel, she reached what she prayed would be her salvation. An old, run-down farmhouse that looked to be surviving the storm about as well as she was. It wasn't much, but even the smallest morsel looks like a feast when you're starving.

She hazarded a knock on the door. Her clothing rippled in the wind, the rain dripping down her hair and across her face. She must have been a pathetic image. She was just beginning to turn away when the door slowly swung open, held mostly closed by a chain lock.

"Who are you?" a man asked, peering through the small slit between the door and the frame. His hair was an unruly mess, sticking up at all angles. One hand rested against the wall next to the door, the other held the handle. Sleep hung in his eyes.

"I need shelter. Please." They were the only words she could get out. The shivering had robbed her of any more than that. Even if she were able to say more, what good would it do?

The man stood in contemplation for a moment. "You can sleep out in the shed. It's not much, but it'll get you through the night."

Serennia nodded a silent thanks, and the man closed the door without another word. She stepped down from the door and tramped through the mud, over to the weather worn building that sat adjacent to the main house. One window was smashed out, jagged shards lining the empty frame. The door pulled against the latch, then slammed back into place, tugged back and forth by the blustering winds. She unlatched it and a gust immediately caught it and flung open hard enough for the hook of the lock to scrape against her finger.

Closing the door behind her took some effort, but after a bit of struggle, she was able to hold it closed long enough to lock it. She pressed her back against the rotting wood, released the breath she'd been holding, and surveyed the night's lodgings. Rain dripped from the cracks in the ceiling and formed pools in the middle of the floor, much of which was covered in hay, blown free from a massive pile that took up most of the back wall. Tools of all kinds lined the other walls, caked in dirt and rust from years of hard use. The conditions reminded her of wandering through the woods as a child, before Lord Hauber had found her. In those days, she'd often snuck into woodsheds to get shelter from the elements.

Now that she was out of the storm, she could focus on the anger that had only grown since leaving Rosewine. How dare Crennel force her out of her home. She had lived there long before he'd sauntered in, and he thought he could force her out because of his own paranoia? How many homes would she be forced out of before she could live in peace? At least Crennel had just wanted her gone. The Arcanaeum had wanted to capture her, to twist and break her until she became a living weapon. If not for them she could still be living a happy life with her parents.

Her emotions ripped out of her in a storm of magical blades that she fired into the haystack, angled low so as not to damage the wall on the other side. The familiar feeling of needles beneath her skin, the one that always accompanied her magic, grew as she continued. She took shot after shot until her arms felt like they were on fire, the pain spreading through her shoulders into her chest. She continued until her arms felt ready to explode, and even then she let loose a couple more for good measure.

It was strange to think that this was the reason for all her misfortune. A gift she wasn't supposed to have, a gift that hurt to use, a gift she had never asked for. She'd gladly have traded it for a peaceful life. All it had ever brought her was pain as she fled from one shitty situation to the next.

Exhausted, she stumbled to the back of the shed, the pain slowly ebbing. The mounds of hay were the best bed she could ask for given the situation, even if it meant a night of itchiness and discomfort. She worked the dried grass into an even pile, pushed some towards the top for a passable pillow, then lay down and struggled to get comfortable. It wasn't much better than the wagon had been, and she knew her body would regret it in the morning. Still, it was likely all that she deserved.

The wind howled outside, the almost rhythmic slamming of the door keeping the sleep at bay though her exhaustion put up a valiant fight. She stared at the stars through the window on the far wall, drawing imaginary constellations between them, until her eyelids at last grew too heavy and shut everything away.

Chapter 3

When morning came, Serennia struggled to get to her feet. Every muscle in her body had seized up from the night spent on a thin bed of straw, and it took some time to coerce them into movement. Once she had worked some life back into her body, a stench assaulted her senses. The signature blend of hay, dirt, and mildew that filled the shed had seemed weaker the night before, kept at bay by her own overwhelming tiredness. She fought back the urge to retch as she made haste for the exit, desperate to get fresh air into her lungs.

She threw open the doors and practically stumbled outside. Remnants of the harsh rains from the night before still lingered. The dirt road that stretched into the horizon was dark and muddy, puddles filling holes and ruts worn by countless wagon wheels over the years. The dwindling wind blew the droplets off the leaves in a steady drip.

Serennia looked southward towards Alcress, completely hidden beyond the horizon. For so long that city had been her world. She felt strange. She had returned to a world she'd thought long behind her, one far more vast and unyielding than the one she'd clung to for so long.

Yet a part of her felt more comfortable in the aggressive unknown than in the cage that Rosewine had become.

She half expected to see Crennel's men marching down the road to track her down and bring her back to the estate, kicking and screaming. Or kill her and bring her body back to Crennel as proof. Either would probably make that man happy. She took a deep breath and reminded herself that she was out of there now. As long as she kept moving, it was over.

In the other direction, the road continued on and vanished among the rolling hills. Serennia considered running. She could continue down the road and leave this sad house far behind her. But kindness was a rare commodity in her life, and a starving person shouldn't refuse what few scraps they're offered.

She didn't have much of a chance to consider her options before the homeowner stepped out from around the building. His hair was more under control than at their first meeting, his eyes vibrant with life. His clothes were already dirty, though Serennia figured much of the grime could have been days or even weeks old.

"Glad to see you're finally awake." The man's voice was fuller now, the sleepy drawl gone. "Half expected you to slip away without a word."

"Thought about it." Serennia wasn't sure what made her tell the truth so blatantly, but something about the man made her feel like she could. She got the feeling that no matter what she said, even if it would sound insane to a normal person, he wouldn't judge her for it. *Better not to test that theory.*

"Well, I'm glad you didn't. Too many people out for themselves these days."

"What do you want me to do?" Serennia knew the kindness wouldn't be free. It almost never was. At least not for her.

"Are you asking about work?" The man scratched the back of his head as he spoke. "Why would I put a young lady like yourself to work?"

Serennia stood in confused silence for a moment. "Because you let me stay here? I owe you something in return, don't I?"

The man chuckled to himself as he shook his head. "I didn't let you stay here because I expected payment. Sometimes good deeds are done for their own sake. Besides, I can't rightly charge for making you sleep in the shed. Those conditions are payment enough."

He reached forward to rest a hand on her shoulder, and Serennia's whole body flinched backward. One of her arms came halfway up to a defensive stance before her rationality kicked in and calmed her nerves. *He's not going to hurt me. He let me stay here for free.*

The man pulled his hand away like he'd just been stung. "Sorry, I didn't mean to startle you."

"It's fine. Sorry." Serennia cast her gaze to the ground, ashamed for the harsh reaction to such a simple gesture. "I'll leave now. Thanks again."

"Nonsense! You're not going anywhere until you've got a full belly." The man turned towards the house and invited her inside with a wide gesture of his arm. "Come on in. My wife will fix you a plate."

Serennia felt like her feet were glued to the ground beneath her. She wanted to move, wanted to follow the kind man inside, wanted to stuff her face with what would probably be the first full meal she'd had in far too long—without it being snuck into her room after hours. Her heart yearned for the warm food, the company, the shelter. But her brain defied her wants. It reminded her that kindness wasn't free, and that she shouldn't take more than she could pay back. After a brief struggle, she pushed her legs into motion and followed the man into his house.

The interior was nothing special: a simple wooden farmhouse with a couple of bedrooms in the back and a kitchen in the far corner. A woman—the man's wife, Serennia assumed—was busy frying something in a pan over the hearth, the sound of crackling fat filling the air. A savoury scent wafted into her nose, reminding Serennia of early mornings spent with Cal in the kitchens at Rosewine.

"My name's Telbek." The man pulled a chair away from the table and indicated it was for Serennia.

"Thank you." She took a hesitant seat and shuffled closer to the table, across from a young boy that was probably half her age, though he was so small he may as well have been a toddler. She realized she hadn't shared her name and chastised herself silently. "I'm Serennia."

"I see our guest has decided to join us for breakfast!" Telbek's wife looked over her shoulder just long enough to see Serennia before she returned her attention to the pan, cracking a handful of eggs that all landed with a sizzle.

"Rost, this is Serennia," Telbek said as he took a seat next to his son. "She's going to be eating breakfast with us, so be nice to her, okay?" Telbek leaned back to watch his wife as she started to scoop the food onto a series of plates.

Serennia felt the young boy's eyes boring into her, searching for answers to questions that hadn't been asked. He was all skin and bones with barely any muscle to fill the space between; his chest hardly made it above the table. Brown hair was cut short atop his head, some patches of it longer than others.

"Why are you in our house?" Rost asked. His eyes remained locked on her, and Serennia covered her torso with crossed arms, hoping she could somehow obscure herself from his vision.

"Your dad invited me in."

"But why are you here? Dad said you were wandering the road all by yourself."

She felt like she had strolled into an interrogation. Like she had committed some kind of crime, and this child was charged with bringing her to justice. "I was travelling." She couldn't help feeling like the boy saw through her lie.

"Were you running from monsters?"

She was, in a sense, though not the bedtime story kind he was thinking of. The child probably imagined her running away from Cinderfolk or witches or some other ridiculous tale made up to scare children into behaving. "Monsters aren't real."

"Rost, stop pestering our guest." Telbek's wife set a plate in front of each of them as she scolded her son. As soon as the food was before her child, his attention shifted from the strange girl sitting across from him to the golden yolks on his plate. "I apologize. He's a very inquisitive little thing. My name's Imra. It's nice to meet you."

"Thank you. It's nice to meet you too." Serennia eyed the plate for a short time. The eggs glistened back at her, the bacon still sizzling from the heat of the pan. She grabbed her fork and dug in, eating with reckless abandon.

"Slow down, you'll make yourself sick eating so fast." Imra settled down with a plate for herself. "Take your time and enjoy the food; it's not going anywhere."

Serennia forced herself to slow her pace, taking time to properly chew each bite. The bacon had the slightest crunch before it gave way to chewiness. The yolks of the eggs were still runny, just the way she had grown to like them. The cooking wasn't as good as Cal's, but then again, Imra wasn't a noble chef.

When the meal was finished, Imra collected the dishes and set them to soak in the wash basin. Serennia sat at the table awkwardly, unsure of whether she was allowed to leave. Her eyes cast around the room until they landed on a sword that leaned against the wall next to the door.

Telbek followed her gaze, then gave a resigned smile and a single, shallow nod. "I used to make a hard living, back when I was a much younger man. It was a difficult life, one that I would be happy to never relive. Still, I can't bring myself to get rid of the sword. I know it would likely fetch a hefty sum, but I feel like the moment I let it go, I'm going to regret it."

Serennia was about to ask him more about his past life when he pivoted the conversation. "Now then, why don't you tell me what you were doing out in that storm? The highway's a dangerous place for a young lady like you, and I doubt you were just on a casual stroll." Telbek leaned forward on his elbows, one hand rested on top of the other.

Could she trust this man? *What a stupid question.* He had given her a place to stay and a full meal for free. Who else could she trust if not someone so generous? "I was fleeing Alcress. I didn't feel like I was safe there anymore."

Telbek's eyes widened, his head slowly nodding as the corners of his lips turned upwards. He pointed a finger at Serennia. "That's where I know you from. You're the Brathis girl." He rolled his eyes and shook his head as laughter escaped his lips. "I don't know how I didn't recognize you earlier!"

"You know me?" Serennia asked, incredulous. She searched through her mind for any recollection of Telbek or Imra but came up blank.

"Well, not personally, of course. I don't think I ever had the chance to actually *meet* you. Did a lot of business in Alcress though, ran into Hauber the odd time, usually walking with you. He always struck me as a nice man. Did business with him once or twice."

"I'm sorry, I don't recall him ever telling me about you."

"Oh, that's no surprise," Telbek said with a dismissive wave of his hand. "Hauber worked with a lot of people, and on top of that he was a secretive man. I'd be shocked if you had heard of most of the people he did business with."

A knock on the front door interrupted any further conversation.

"Hello? We're here on behalf of Lord Brathis of Alcress. We'd like to speak with you a moment."

Serennia jumped to her feet, frantically scanning the room for anywhere she could hide. She should have known they'd come looking for her. After what she'd done to Crennel of course they wouldn't just let her go. "They can't find me."

"This way. With me." Imra grabbed Serennia by the arm and towed her to the back of the house and into the bedroom. The woman slid the bed out of the way, revealing a trapdoor. "Hide down here. I'll get you when it's safe."

Serennia didn't spare a single thought to protest. She flung open the wooden hatch and jumped down, landing hard on the ground below. The only light came from four glowstones, one in each corner, revealing walls of hard-packed dirt. The room was wide enough that Serennia could lie with her arms above her head and not touch either side.

The door closed above. She heard the scraping of the bed being moved back into place, followed by Imra's footsteps moving back into the main room. The conversation above her was only faint whispers, muted beyond the point of comprehension. She strained to listen, hoping to make out anything that might indicate how it was going, but it was a pointless effort.

Serennia's nerves raced out of control as she paced around the small room. Her heart beat so loudly she thought she could hear it echoing around her. Would Crennel's men think to check beneath the bed? How much time would have to pass before they allowed her back out?

Footsteps traced a path around the house, more than could belong to just Telbek and Imra. *Please let them be okay.* They'd be fine. Crennel's men wouldn't stoop so low as to kill innocents. *They tried to kill me less than a day ago.* No. She couldn't think like that. She gripped the pendant in her pocket so tightly she was afraid she'd break it.

How long had it been since she'd hidden? Minutes? Hours? Serennia half sat, half fell to the ground, her breathing heavy. She wrapped her arms around her knees with her head down, trying in vain to focus on anything that might stop her mind from spinning with all the possibilities of what could have happened above.

When at last the trap door opened again, the light that spilled in was blinding. Serennia blinked her eyes against the luminous assault, wondering whose face it would be staring down at her. Once her vision finally adjusted, she was relieved to see Telbek.

"Sorry to cram you in there like that." He reached down and grabbed her arm, hauling her back up with some help from Imra. "We didn't have any other options on such short notice."

"It's okay. I appreciate the help. Those men would have killed me otherwise."

Imra's eyes went wide, but Telbek only nodded. "There's a lot more going on at that estate than people realize, isn't there? I've heard grumbling from the former staff that the place had taken a turn for the worse since Crennel took over, but I never thought it could be so bad."

"He's a monster," Serennia said, her emotion somewhere distant. "Someone tried to poison him last night, and he blames me. He tried to kill me, so I fought back and left him seriously injured. I need to go before his thugs come back. I don't want you getting hurt if they find me here."

"Where are you going to go?" Imra asked.

"Ruddreth, I think. At least for now." She remembered the wagon driver had been headed there, and it seemed as good a destination as any. Lord Hauber had often travelled to Ruddreth for business, though she'd never gone with him. Any time he returned, he would always complain about how chaotic and messy the city was. If there was anywhere she could hide from Crennel and his men, that would be the place.

"Ruddreth can be a dangerous city for newcomers. Are you sure you know what you're getting yourself into?" Telbek had a point, yet what choice did she have?

"I'll be fine. Lord Hauber taught me how to defend myself in case of emergencies."

Telbek gave her a slow nod, and she wondered if he knew more about her than he was letting on. "If that's the case, then at least let me take you there. We can avoid the highway, at least for the next day or so. I'll bring some wares to sell at the markets, so if we are spotted we won't look suspicious. Besides, it will get you there a lot faster."

"You don't have to do this, Telbek," Serennia said. If he got caught transporting her, there was no telling what Crennel's men would do to him.

"If you go out there on your own, you'll more than likely get caught long before you make it to Ruddreth. The least I can do is give you a fighting chance. Besides"—Telbek nodded his head toward the trapdoor—"I have some experience with this sort of thing."

Chapter 4

Despite the horrors and scars left by her years at Rosewine, a small part of Serennia preferred the known monster to the crushing unknowingness she now faced. Ruddreth loomed in the distance, the worn buildings on its outskirts closing in, ready to engulf her. The sunlight sparkled off the water of the bay behind it.

If two large, cluttered cities could truly be opposites, Ruddreth and Alcress were perfect examples. Alcress had been built with careful deliberation, extensively planned by experts to maximize efficient usage of land. Each new district was square and uniform, divided by straight intersecting streets. It was impossible to get lost because she knew where each turn would lead her.

Ruddreth was more circular and chaotic. The city had been built outward from the West Bay, new houses and shops added in wherever they'd fit. The roads were winding and confusing, criss-crossing back and forth over each other as they worked their way through the brickwork jungle. Beggars lined the streets of the outer rim, the more fortunate among them sitting on rags. Their clothing—most of which was tattered and torn beyond recognition—was saturated with stains and grime. The acrid scent of so many unwashed, dying bodies crowding the streets pushed Serennia to the brink of sickness.

"It's rough, the first time. You never quite learn how to tune it out." Telbek must have noticed Serennia's discomfort, because he rested a placating hand on her shoulder. The gesture made her flinch again, though she managed to keep it more controlled than the previous time. *Calm down. You can't keep jumping like a damn stray cat every time someone gets too close to you.*

The two of them had managed to make it all the way to Ruddreth without any trouble. The two-day wagon ride had been rough, but Serennia was at last beginning to feel a sense of safety. They didn't know if their avoidance of Crennel's men had been luck or if he had called off the search. Either way, she was grateful.

"Soon enough we'll be out of the outer ring. Then the city won't be so bad." Telbek's words did nothing to assuage her worries. The more she looked around, the harder it was to imagine the city getting any better.

The buildings were chipped and falling apart, the roads rocky and uneven. The only solace she found was the near assuredness of her safety within the mess that sprouted around her. Even if Crennel sent men to look for her, there were far too many places for her to hide in the sprawling brick and mortar that was Ruddreth.

The wagon bumped and rattled down what passed for a road until the more dismal aspects of the town began to fade away. Houses started to show more evidence of upkeep, and the homeless people begging along the roadsides became fewer and farther between. The overwhelming stench of human rot was slowly replaced by the scent of fresh food, even if the undertone of garbage still floated somewhere in the distance. People smiled more than in the outer ring, Serennia noticed, the look of hunger in their eyes virtually nonexistent. They all seemed so fake.

"This should be far enough," Telbek said. "Always better to set up as close to the inner ring as possible. Keeps you away from most of the thieves. The Five curse me if those damn Sparrows take any more of my goods."

"Sparrows?" Serennia asked. She had a hard time understanding why a man like Telbek would have a problem with a bunch of birds.

"A group of no-good thieves who prowl Ruddreth and steal anything they can get their hands on. The locals have grown wise to their tricks, so they tend to prey on the travelling merchants who don't know any better."

Serennia couldn't imagine such a thing. Alcress had thieves, sure, but an organized group of them working together? She'd never heard of anything like it. Then again, it wasn't like she had much experience with cities.

"It looks like this is where we part ways, kid," Telbek said as he brought the wagon to a halt. He climbed down from his seat, then offered a hand to Serennia to help her down. "Are you sure this is where you wanna start calling home?"

Serennia looked at the various buildings around her, cropping up wherever there was space. She could feel her nerves like a clenched fist around her heart. "I think so, yeah."

"I'm going to set up shop right here, so you know where to find me if you change your mind in the next few hours. And if you ever find yourself needing a break from the city, you're always welcome at the farm."

"Thanks." Serennia gave Telbek a quick nod before she set off down the road. After a couple of steps, she hesitated and looked over her shoulder towards the man who had opened his home to her. "For everything," she added.

Telbek responded with a nod and a tip of his hat before he redirected his attention to setting up shop. Before she got far, he called out to her again. "There's a kitchen a little ways down this street that serves free food to the less fortunate. If you're hungry, I recommend stopping in. The food's good, plus they're open all day and I know a couple of the volunteers. If you end up visiting, tell them I sent you."

Serennia laughed, more to herself than out loud. "Will do, thanks." She wandered down the street, headed in the direction of the kitchen. Her stomach had been grumbling for some time now, unsatisfied by the quick breakfast of bread and cured meats she had shared with Telbek before they set out at dawn.

As far as Serennia could tell, the inner and outer parts of the city were divided by a bustling thoroughfare which ran in an arch from one side of the bay to the other. She found the kitchen situated between houses and storefronts on the inner-city side of the road. The smell of warm meat and vegetables wafted through the air, reminding her of evenings spent chatting with Cal in the kitchen. She pushed those memories away. Cal was out of her life now, and dwelling would only make it hurt more.

When she stepped inside, Serennia was amazed by the cleanliness of it. While it wasn't a polished gem by any stretch, the floors were swept clear of any obvious debris, and most of the windows were unbroken, save for one that was boarded up on the far side—more than could be said for the buildings around it.

A long counter stretched almost the full length of the back wall, with stations set up at regular intervals for stock pots to nestle into. Only half of them were filled, hardly enough for the lunch rush that would no doubt be coming. One volunteer was ladling soup into an awaiting bowl, while the other three wiped down their areas and stirred idly while they chatted with their fellows.

"Good timing, we just opened," a volunteer said. "Grab a bowl and come on up."

Just opened? So much for being open all day. Serennia helped herself to a bowl from the stack near the entrance. She brought the dish up to one of the unoccupied workers, unsure of the protocol. Did she just hold out the bowl to them? Was she supposed to ask nicely? It wasn't until she was almost to the counter that she considered the possibility of each pot being a different kind of soup.

The worker straight ahead must have noticed her wandering eyes. "They're all the same; no need to worry about your choices." He spoke without a hint of judgment in his voice, only comfort and hospitality. "Just come on up and I'll fill your bowl."

Serennia finished crossing the distance between her and the counter, her bowl held up in both hands. The man ladled in a healthy portion of soup, which seemed to be some kind of amalgamation of whatever meats and vegetables had been available. Not that she was one to judge. If she was any hungrier, she might have eaten the bowl.

"You new here in Ruddreth?" the man asked. "I don't think I've seen your face in here before." His greying hair fell almost to his shoulders, matched by a scraggly beard that looked like it hadn't seen a comb in its life.

"Just got here today." Serennia wasn't sure how much information to give the man. She doubted someone working at an outer city soup kitchen was a threat to her, but she had no idea how far Crennel's eyes and ears extended. Then again, if this man was working for Crennel, he surely would have recognized her. Crennel would have provided everyone with descriptions of her, and her looks weren't exactly common in these parts.

"Where are you from?" The man seemed to pick up on her apprehension, because he quickly followed up his question. "If you don't mind me asking, of course."

Serennia debated for a moment. How much could she trust people she'd never met? However, Lord Hauber had been a stranger once, and he ended up being one of the kindest people in her life. So had Telbek.

She decided to give the man the benefit of the doubt. If he *was* working for Crennel, he'd already know the answer anyway. "I'm from Alcress."

Something in the man's eyes lit up. A spike of worry shot through her system. Was he working for Crennel after all? Had his questions been a ploy to confirm her identity before he went after her?

"So that's where I know you from. You're Hauber's girl, aren't you? I don't know how I didn't recognize you right away!" Those words hit Serennia like a wave of relief. Not only was he not working for Crennel, but by the sounds of it, he was an old friend of Lord Hauber's.

"Yeah, I am." She wanted to say more, but the words wouldn't come, arrested by her irrational fear of what might happen if she gave any more details.

The man behind the counter rested his ladle on the edge of the pot, then circled around to her side. When he reached her, he took the bowl from her, set it down, and wrapped her in a hug before she fully knew what was happening.

"It pained me to hear of his death. The world lost a great man that day. I can only imagine how hard that must have been for you."

Serennia felt tears push against the corners of her eyes and had to fight them down. She wasn't about to cry in public, much less surrounded by complete strangers. She knew she should say something to ease the man's mind, yet any time she tried to talk the tears threatened to return.

After a short time, the man released her and took a step back. "My name's Ralsin. I was a good friend of Lord Hauber's, and I intend to be every bit a friend to his kin." Ralsin paused and tilted his head to one side, like he'd just remember an important detail. "Well, most of his kin, anyway. Crennel can turn to ash for all I care."

An unexpected laugh burst out of Serennia's lungs. It was nice to hear someone else held the same contempt for the new Lord Brathis as she did. "Why do you think I ran away?" she said, the last vestiges of laughter still playing across her words.

"Is there anything I can do to help you out?" Ralsin's tone had returned to a more serious note. "I know surviving in this city can be rough at the best of times."

Serennia considered his offer. Now that she'd found the kitchen, food was more or less taken care of. The only other thing she'd need would be some kind of shelter, though she doubted he could provide that. She wouldn't want to live with a man she had only just met, and there was no way she'd let him pay for her to have a room, either. Still, it couldn't hurt to ask.

Ralsin stroked his beard as he thought. After a few seconds, he nodded to himself. "A couple of blocks down the road there's an inn called the Albatross. Ask for Amira, she's the owner. Tell her you're Lord Hauber's daughter, and that I sent you."

"I don't want you paying for my room or anything," Serennia said. "I appreciate the offer, but I can manage on my own."

Ralsin chuckled and held up his hands. "Don't worry, I'm not offering to cover your expenses. Believe it or not, this volunteer job doesn't pay very well. Lord Hauber used to stay at the Albatross whenever he came to town. He bought one of the rooms off Amira. He became the permanent owner, and last I heard, she was still honouring that purchase."

"I hope that's the case. Thank you. I appreciate your help."

Ralsin waved his hand dismissively. "No need to thank me. Like I said, Hauber was a good friend of mine, and I'm happy to help his kid. Did you know Hauber used to volunteer at this kitchen whenever he was in town?"

Serennia had never heard that before, but it didn't surprise her. Back home he would always do anything he could to help the less fortunate. She was more surprised he'd had any money left for himself with how much he donated to the lower class.

Ralsin bid her goodbye and returned to his station behind the counter as a line of hungry faces came through the door. Serennia claimed an empty table nearby and dug into her food, each spoonful a welcome warmth in her stomach. It may not have been a gourmet meal but, compared to the scraps she had been living on, it tasted like it was fit for a king. When her spoon clacked against the bottom of the bowl, she knew she'd be coming back.

Chapter 5

The inside of the Albatross was exactly as Serennia had pictured it, as though the designer had read about inns from a book and copied everything word for word. A bar counter dominated one side, behind which a stout woman washed cups and took orders. A door behind her led to the kitchen, judging by the sounds and smells that poured through it. The rest of the room was filled with round tables ringed by chairs, half of which were filled with patrons, some of them already drunk despite the freshness of the afternoon.

Serennia felt out of her depth. Something told her they would know she didn't belong and try to throw her out. A couple of them looked at her when she entered, their wandering eyes and half-closed gazes piercing right through her, despite none of their stares lingering for more than a fraction of a second. Before her anxiety could take hold of her, she walked up to the bar and waited to catch the woman's attention.

"Excuse me," Serennia said when the woman at last looked her way. "I'm looking for Amira. Is she in today?"

The woman grinned and set down the glass she'd been cleaning. "You're looking at her. What can I do for you?"

Serennia swallowed hard. Amira only came up to her collar, but she was built like an ox and had the presence of someone twice her height. Her dusky skin implied Garleshi heritage, the same as Serennia's birth parents. Her white hair was beginning to lose some of its starkness, the greying strands pulled back into a loose bun. Her sharp, hardened eyes were only marginally softened by the smile that beamed beneath them.

"I'm Lord Hauber's daughter. Ralsin told me to come here and ask about my dad's old room." She'd meant it to be a statement, but the last sentence came out more like a question. She took deep breaths in the hopes it would calm her nerves.

"Lord Hauber's daughter, huh?" Amira picked up another glass and wiped the rim with her rag. The muscles in her arm flexed with each rotation of the cup, so much so that Serennia half expected her sleeves to rip under the pressure. "No offence, but you don't look much like a noble's daughter, much less related to Hauber Brathis."

"My mother was Garleshi; I take after her. As for the rest of my appearance, it's been a long few years since my father's death."

Amira set down the glass and slung the rag over her shoulder. "Well, if Ralsin sent you, then I'm inclined to believe you're telling the truth. Not sure why I bothered keeping old Hauber's room clear all this time, but I suppose it's good that I did." She grabbed a key from under the counter and slid it to Serennia. "End of the hall. Try not to wreck the place."

"Thank you." Serennia took the key and pocketed it, as if it was some kind of secret from the rest of the patrons. Amira went back to taking orders and serving drinks. Serennia knew a cue to leave when she saw one.

The staircase that led to the rooms took up a good portion of the back wall. They looked like they hadn't been repaired since they were first built, each step drawing an awful creak from boards that were almost certainly older than she was. Doors lined either side of the hallways upstairs, sounds murmuring from some of them that Serennia did her best to ignore. At the end of the hall, her door sat facing her like an ominous destiny.

When she slid the key into the lock and let herself into the room, the first thing that hit her was the musty smell. She wondered how long it had been since anyone had been inside, much less opened a window and aired the place out. Dust floated in the air, visible in the beams of sunlight that pierced through the lone window.

The room was sparsely furnished, though more than enough for her needs. There was a simple bed across from the door, and a writing desk underneath the window. In the middle was a small table with four chairs pushed in around it, the surface marred with scratches and stains. There was even a trunk at the foot of the bed where she could put her belongings—once she acquired some.

Serennia stepped in and closed the door behind her, ensuring the lock was in place before she allowed herself to relax. It wasn't much, and it definitely needed fixing up, but it was hers. A place that was wholly her own, where she didn't have to worry about Crennel Brathis barging in and making demands of her.

She fell onto the bed, the mattress firmer than the one at Rosewine, yet still much softer than she'd expected. She let out a breath she felt like she'd been holding in since Alcress. For the first time in months, perhaps even years, she felt the tension leave her body, like a weight lifted from her soul. A part of her wanted to cry.

Serennia turned around and leaned back, her elbows resting on the desk behind her. She gave the room a quick scan as she made a mental note of the work she'd need to do. Every bit of furniture needed to be dusted, the floor could do with a good sweep, and who knew how old the sheets on the bed were. As she surveyed the area, she noticed a hatch of some kind built into the ceiling. She slid the trunk underneath it, which gave her just enough extra height to reach it.

A clear sky greeted her when she pushed open the hatch. She put the trunk back where she'd found it, instead standing on the table so that her shoulder poked through the opening. With a jump, she was able to pull herself up onto the roof of the Albatross. Wind rippled across her clothing, her hair dancing behind her. Few buildings in the area were taller than the inn, so the rooftop gave her a great view of the surrounding city. People bustled around on the streets below, hurrying from place to place like time was running out.

She had forgotten what freedom felt like. Years cooped up in Rosewine had robbed her of so many simple feelings: the fresh air, the sunlight, even the feeling of something other than hardwood or carpet beneath her feet. She didn't realize how much she had missed those things until she had them back.

Serennia was unsure of how much time had passed when she finally returned to her room. As much as she would have liked to spend the whole day up there, she couldn't afford to stop yet. She still had her entire life to figure out. Before anything else, she would have to get a job. How else could she hope to survive in Ruddreth without becoming one of the disparate beggars that filled the outer city?

The feet of the table scraped against the wooden floor as she pushed it back into its place. She checked for any signs of scratches on the hardwood, hoping she had left it undamaged so as not to draw the wrath of Amira. The woman looked fit enough to toss her all the way out of Ruddreth.

As she scanned the floor, a folded piece of paper drew her eyes. It was only a couple of feet from the doorway, likely from someone sliding it underneath the frame while she had been up on the roof. Her heart beat like a hammer. A thousand possibilities swirled in her mind as to who might be responsible, from Crennel's goons to the people that had hunted her when she was a child.

With trembling hands, she picked up the paper and unfolded it. The page turned out to be a letter addressed to her, which only made her more anxious.

Serennia,

You deserve better than to waste away in Ruddreth like the other hopefuls who come only to become beggars. Your life needs purpose, and that is something I would be happy to provide. I see great potential in you, and I will do anything in my power to help you realize it. Come to the kitchen for dinner tonight and we can meet.

-Genn

By the time her eyes reached the bottom of the letter her hands were shaking so much she thought she would tear the paper. Sweat dripped down her forehead, her mouth dry. She swallowed hard. Who was this person? How did they know where she was living so soon after she moved in? More importantly, what did they want with her?

Be rational. The odds that this Genn person is involved with the Arcanaeum are almost zero. She tried to reassure herself that this wasn't related to her previous traumatic experiences. She told herself that whoever had written the letter was legitimately trying to help her. Besides, how long could she hope to survive in the city on her own? She knew nothing about living in a place as sprawling as Ruddreth. A place to stay was a good start, but it wasn't like she could spend every day hanging out in the Albatross. Someone that could help her, someone that knew the city, could be a huge benefit. She thought of everything she could to convince herself that Genn had her best interests at heart, that they would somehow make her life in Ruddreth less daunting.

Nothing she did calmed the nerves that raged under her skin.

* * * * *

A few hours after inheriting the room at the Albatross, Serennia left its comfort to roam the streets of Ruddreth. It was remarkable the way the city was so neatly divided between rich and poor. She wondered why the local police didn't enforce their laws through the whole city instead of stopping at the main thoroughfare. Were they spread too thin? Or did they just not care about the outer half?

Whatever the reason, Serennia stuck to the poorer side of the road. It was easier to avoid drawing attention in the outer city, where just about everyone was too focused on their own survival to worry about anyone else. As long as she kept her head down and didn't walk too fast, nobody paid her any attention.

Her hand went to the pendant in her pocket. It was the only thing she had left from her old life, though a part of her wondered why she bothered keeping it. She couldn't help feeling it was pointless to keep carrying it around. It wasn't like she was ever going to wear it again.

Still, she clutched it tight enough that the metal dug into her palm, hoping—perhaps foolishly—that it would calm her beating heart.

Before long she pushed through the door to the soup kitchen and was greeted by the friendly faces behind the counter. Most of the volunteers were different from the ones earlier in the day, though she supposed that was normal. They likely worked in shifts, rotating between meals.

Serennia grabbed her bowl, walked up to the counter, and got served two ladles full of some kind of stew, filled with chunks of meat and hearty vegetables. The scent tugged at her stomach, encouraging what little appetite she had.

She turned and looked across the room, searching for anyone that might be Genn. Her eyes met those of a man who couldn't have been much older than herself. He sat alone at a table on the far side of the building, facing the entrance. His dishevelled, shoulder-length hair obscured his face, partially covering eyes that felt like they looked through her. He gave a shallow, almost imperceptible nod.

Serennia drew in a deep breath and took her first hesitant step towards the man. The closer she got, the more her heart raged in her chest, her breath coming in shaky inhales. *It's not too late to turn back.* She knew this, yet at the same time, she knew it wasn't an option. She had come too far. He had seen her face and knew where she lived. Her only choice was to see things through.

"Genn, I assume?" Serennia placed her bowl on the table and sat down, the feet of the chair screeching along the floor as she pulled herself in.

"Genn had prior obligations, I'm afraid." The man ate a spoonful of his stew, savouring the food longer than Serennia would have liked. "Consider me an authorized messenger." He continued to work on his dinner, his eyes fixated on the bowl in front of him.

Serennia sat in silence, waiting for him to open the conversation. It seemed like the man across from her had forgotten she was there, judging by the way he focused intently on his bowl, eating spoonful after spoonful, savouring every bite. She wondered why Genn would invite her and not show. Was this a test of some kind? Or had something truly come up?

After a couple of minutes of uncomfortable silence, the man spoke again. "I don't know about you, but I'm hungry. And I don't like talking business on an empty stomach. Now you don't have to eat yours, but I intend to finish mine, so you might as well take the opportunity to do the same."

Eating was the furthest thing from Serennia's mind. Her stomach felt like it was clenched in a fist, squeezing tighter with each passing second. She resigned herself to trying to eat, hoping it might lessen her discomfort. The first couple of mouthfuls were a chore. Her brain didn't want to think about dinner, and her arms were reluctant to raise the spoon. As the flavours settled in, eating got easier, until she was eagerly filling her stomach with the delicious meal. She hadn't realized such simple food could be so *satisfying*.

When she was halfway finished, she noticed the man raise his head. He didn't look at her, instead observing the room around them, but she felt unsettled all the same.

She set her spoon down and looked up, disappointed that she wouldn't be able to finish her meal.

"Please, finish your dinner," the man said when he realized she was watching him. "It's important to be well fed. I wouldn't have you going hungry on my account."

Try as she might to eat the remainder of her stew, Serennia's stomach had restricted itself again. Her next couple of swallows felt like she was working against a current. Finally, she sat her spoon down, leaving the last dregs untouched, and sat up in her chair.

The man eyed her, and a smirk turned up the corner of his lips. "I suppose I should start by introducing myself. My name's Taza."

Serennia expected some sort of greeting gesture to follow, but Taza's hands didn't move from where they were laced in front of him. Feeling her manners from Rosewine kick in, she responded. "My name's Serennia."

"A pleasure," Taza said with a nod. "Now tell me, why are you here?"

Serennia's brow furrowed, her eyes glancing from side to side as if the answer might be lurking in her periphery. "Genn invited me here? He slid a letter under my door. I assumed he had told you."

"Yes, I'm aware of the letter. But that doesn't tell me why you came. You had a choice, after all."

"I'm not sure I did."

"Don't be foolish, Serennia. You always have a choice. Choices are what make us human and separate us from more base creatures. Even now, you have a choice. You could walk away right now and face no consequences. I can't promise we won't try to contact you again, but you would be free to ignore us without repercussions."

She considered that option for a moment. She had an out. If she got up and left, then her life could continue, unchanged. *Do I really want that, though? And who's to say these people will stick to their word?*

"I'm already here. The least I can do is hear you out."

"I'm happy to hear that." Taza leaned forward, his next words just above a whisper. "What do you know about the Sparrows?"

Serennia thought back to when she'd arrived earlier that morning. "The thieves? All I know is that they steal from merchants in the outer ring."

Taza let a sharp breath out his nose. "I suppose they do, though there is much more to them than that. Tell me, Serennia. What are your first impressions of Ruddreth?"

Is he serious? She hadn't even been in the city for a full day; how was she supposed to have any kind of opinion on the place? He looked at her with expectation, and she knew he wouldn't accept anything less than a proper answer.

"The city seems...divided? I've never heard of a place where the rich and the poor are so obviously kept apart."

"Unfortunately, class division is common in big cities like this. However, in my experience, nowhere is that division stronger than here in Ruddreth. The Sparrows aim to change that."

"By stealing produce from local farmers? Seems to me like you're on the side of the rich."

"I can see how our outward actions might give that impression. I assure you, though, that the Sparrows are about much more than petty theft. We need to put up a facade for the powerful. So long as they see us as a problem only for the outer city, they won't suspect us when we go after larger prey."

"So what *are* you about, then?"

"We want to knock the nobility off their pedestals, so to speak. By stripping them of their means to feel superior, we can create true equality. A city where people aren't forced into a life of hardship simply for being born on the wrong side of the street."

Serennia thought back to Lord Hauber, giving an enviable life to a young girl he found shivering in the cold for no reason other than simple generosity. Did these Sparrows know that there were good nobles out there? Or would they paint them all with the same brush and name them all a problem? Then her thoughts shifted until she saw herself running down a hallway, fearing for her life in a place that had once been her home.

"So why approach me?" Serennia asked, fighting to banish the intrusive memories. The pain lessened, though she could still feel it somewhere in the recesses of her brain.

"We are always on the lookout for those who might be sympathetic to our cause. Many of the locals are too downtrodden to believe things could ever be better. But an outsider such as yourself doesn't have such concerns."

Taza reached into his coat and produced a letter, which he set on the table and slid towards Serennia with one hand. It was sealed with a circle of wax, imprinted with the silhouette of a bird in flight. She took the letter in one hand and looked it over.

"If what I've said resonates with some part of you, then open the letter in the privacy of your room. Inside you'll find instructions on what you must do to join the Sparrows."

"What if I'm not interested?" Serennia set the letter down and placed her hands in her lap, hoping Taza hadn't noticed how much they trembled.

"If you decide you don't want to be part of our solution, you are welcome to live your life. Whichever you choose, burn the letter when you're finished."

Taza stood from his seat without waiting for any further response. He gathered up his dishes and started for the door but hesitated beside her.

"We look forward to your decision."

A moment later, he was gone, leaving Serennia with the letter and countless questions.

Chapter 6

Serennia looked up at the wall that surrounded Tulkarr Manor and wondered if she was about to make a mistake. The job seemed simple enough, but as the estate loomed above her, she couldn't help feeling like she was in over her head. Did she really want to join the Sparrows this badly?

She remembered the first year after Crennel had taken over Rosewine, when she used to sneak out to roam the city while he was busy. Those days had felt so exhilarating. Afternoons spent with her nerves racing, evenings yearning to tell people what she'd accomplished, barely having the willpower to keep the secret. Crennel had caught her, putting those days to a stop after. She'd grown too confident, slipped up a single time, and he'd responded by increasing security around the property.

If the Five favoured her, she'd have retained some of those skills.

A quick scan of her surroundings revealed a tree on the far edge of the property. One of the limbs was within an arm's length of a window and, with any luck, it would be strong enough to support her weight. She stuck to the shadows as she crossed the distance, ducking behind bushes and shrubs to keep out of sight. A couple of guards were in the distance, walking around the topiary garden that sprawled out from the front of the house. She let out a breath of relief when neither of them turned around before she was out of sight.

At the base of the tree, the difficulty of her task began to dawn on her. The tree had no low-hanging branches. They looked like they'd all been sawn off, likely to prevent people from attempting exactly what she was about to do. Unfortunately for them, it would take a lot more than that to stop her. She couldn't help wondering what Lord Hauber would think if he knew what she was about to do with the powers he'd spent so long training her to use.

Arcane blades formed around her fingertips, each one half as long as her fingers. She stabbed at the trunk and the claws dug in deep, splintering the bark. Putting one foot against the rough wood, she pushed upward and slammed the other hand into the tree. Step by step, she worked her way to the top, her arms straining as she pulled herself up. By the time she reached a branch, sweat was starting to bead on her forehead.

There was no time to rest. Her climbing hadn't been the quietest thing in the world, and she didn't want to hang around to find out if the guards had heard her. A few short jumps took her to the limb she'd spotted from the ground, which she tested with a couple of hesitant steps while still gripping a thicker branch above her. When it didn't crack beneath her feet, she began inching across, ever closer to the point of no return.

The window was locked, which came as no surprise. A quick arcane blade took care of that, slashing through the lock and rendering it useless. The window was just far enough away that she had to reach out at full extension, causing her heartbeat to quicken, her ankles gripping the limb of the tree with every bit of strength she had. Her torso hung perilously in the air as she swung open the window.

Serennia drew in a deep breath, knowing the next part would be tricky. She gripped the inside of the windowsill with both hands, her muscles straining as she stretched them to their limit, her feet already slipping from where they kept her anchored to the tree. With a silent prayer to anyone who might be listening, Serennia let go with her legs and let them drop beneath her. Her lower half slammed against the wall of the manor, the force almost enough to make her lose her grip. She managed to hang on and pull herself up, her feet gaining purchase on the brick wall.

She'd done it. She'd snuck into Tulkarr Manor without being spotted. A part of her wanted to celebrate, to rejoice in a job well done, but she restrained herself. That had been the easy part. The true challenge had just begun.

She seemed to have landed herself in a bedroom, though the level of orderliness implied it was an unused guest room. At least, she hoped it was. She made her way to the door and pressed her ear against it, listening for any guards that might be walking the halls outside. She was met with only silence, so she opened the door.

Tulkarr Manor reminded Serennia so much of Rosewine Estate that her cheek stung just thinking about it. It had the same air of nobility, the same evidence of frivolous spending. Even the carpet felt the same beneath her feet. She'd seen siblings that looked less alike than these two damned mansions. *Don't pay attention to the similarities. Focus on the job at hand. Get in, get out. Simple as that.*

She hoped it was late enough that Lord Tulkarr would be fast asleep. According to the letter, most of his bodyguards were placed in strategic positions around the yard, keeping a vigilant eye out for would-be intruders.

As Serennia prowled the hallways, she looked around in disgust at the treasures placed so casually around the room. Hand-fired vases, golden candle holders, masterful paintings hanging on the wall. So many treasures that would be so easy to take. She nabbed a couple of smaller riches and stuffed them into a small pouch tied around her waist. A crystal dish, some jewellery left out on end tables. As much as she hated the arrogance of the affluent, it sure made things easier when they left their valuables lying around.

The resemblance between Tulkarr Manor and Rosewine might have haunted her, but it meant that she had a pretty good idea where the master bedroom was. She crept down the halls, her steps slow and silent. At the end of the hall, she found the room exactly where she had expected. Two bodyguards stood alert, one on either side of the door. They hadn't noticed her, though she didn't know how long that would last.

Serennia inched as close as she dared, keeping a careful watch on the guards in case one of them saw her. She hid behind a small table that stood against the wall, searching for any weakness she could take advantage of.

A thick hand clasped over her mouth, fingers digging into her cheek. Another hand reached around her chest and grabbed her arm as she was lifted off the ground.

"Well, well. What do we have here?" The man's breath was hot against the back of her neck. Her own breath quickened as she fought every urge to swing her arms and legs in self defence. "Someone trying to steal from Lord Tulkarr, huh?"

His voice attracted the attention of the door guards, who craned their necks to see the struggle unfolding in the darkness. The man holding Serennia stepped into the light, bringing her into view of his partners. "What do you think we should do with her?"

"I say we lock her up and let her rot."

"Why waste the cell? Just kill her now and get it over with."

Fear sank in. Serennia grabbed the wrist of the man restraining her and tried to pull herself free, but her strength was no match for a man twice her size.

"Nice try, kid. But I'm afraid you're not getting out of here unless I say so." The man chortled, his spit splattering against her. The other guards joined in, snickering under their breath.

There was nobody to save her. She was all alone. Memories of Rosewine flooded her mind until Crennel's face replaced those of the men swarming her. Tears streamed out of the corners of her eyes and dropped onto the meaty hand that covered her face.

"Aww, little thing's crying. What's wrong? Scared of what we'll do to you?" His body shook with laughter.

She knew she could get out of this, but she hated the thought of it. She could still see the corpses of the Rosewine guards, Crennel's blood on her clothes. It was the oldest rule of nature: kill or be killed. Her hands trembled, the sweat beading on her forehead. The men continued to jeer at her, their words a dull rumble in her ears. *I don't want to do this. I don't want to do this.*

One of them threw a punch into her stomach, almost hard enough to force the air from her lungs. Her body tried to double over, but she was held too tightly by her captor. Bile rose from her gut, clawing at the inside of her throat, barely held down through a mix of willpower and the inability to open her mouth.

Another fist followed the first, this time from the other guard, and Serennia clenched her teeth against the pain. If she hadn't already been crying, tears would have welled in her eyes. She tried to punch the guard who had just struck her, only to have her blow connect with open air.

Eyes closed, she squeezed back the tears and pressed her hand against the elbow of the man holding her. An instant later, she heard the unmistakable sound of the ethereal blade slicing through his arm. The sickening noise lingered in her ears. She pulled her hand away as his warm blood gushed against it, disgusted by the wet feeling between her fingers. She dropped to the ground and put distance between herself and her aggressors as fast as she could.

"Curse you!" He held his arm in a futile attempt to stem the flow of blood.

"Shut up! You're going to wake Lord Tulkarr!" one of the other guards warned in a hushed yell.

"The hell do you expect? She just punched a hole through my damn arm!"

"How about you keep your mouth shut and help us kill this arrogant little child!"

The three men grouped up and walked towards her, shoulder to shoulder. Retreat wasn't an option. If she left without accomplishing her task, Taza might decide to punish her for risking their operation.

The guard that had been holding her lunged forward, his entire body weight behind his shoulder as it slammed into her chest. Serennia was forced backward into the table she had been hiding behind earlier, its edge driving hard into her back, sending a jolt along her spine.

All three of them drew their swords as they closed in on her, taking advantage of her disorientation. *It's now or never.*

Serennia held her hands out, closed her eyes, and turned her head away from the men that slowly approached her. Every inch of her skin cringed as she heard the sound of blades on flesh that was becoming all too familiar. She opened her eyes and tried not to look at the guards. She knew what she would find.

She hated that she could take away lives so easily. Hated how often she was having to resort to her magic. Most of all, she hated that it hurt a little less every time. The idea that she could so easily deal with three men that could physically overpower her was strangely reassuring. She smothered those feelings.

Serennia gave herself a moment to catch her breath. Everything above her waist throbbed with pain, her heart beating so hard she worried it might bruise her ribs. She leaned against the wall, one hand gripping her stomach, and willed the pain to fade. After a handful of seconds she exhaled, steeled herself, and stepped over the bodies that lay crumpled on the ground, ignoring the sounds of the dying.

The double doors to Lord Tulkarr's bedroom opened almost without a sound. The room inside was opulent, as she'd expected. The bed was larger than any she had ever seen, cornered by four twisting pillars that extended to the ceiling. Violet draperies hung between them, matching the velvet curtains that framed the picture window. Paintings and tapestries adorned the walls, the desk and cabinets topped with the finest jewels Serennia had ever seen. A vast rug was splayed out across the floor, reaching almost from wall to wall.

And there, on the nightstand, was the ring. A golden band beset with a diamond the size of Serennia's thumbnail. It sat on a plush pillow, just asking to be stolen. Next to it was an arcane ring: an opal stone on a bronze band. She hadn't realized Tulkarr had studied at the Arcanaeum. It wasn't unusual for nobles to take some basic lessons in magic, though most that did lived in the northeast, closer to the Arcanaeum.

Serennia crept to his bedside and pocketed both rings. The gold one she would give to Taza as proof of a successful mission, but the arcane ring was hers. After everything she'd gone through so far, she deserved payment.

Lord Tulkarr continued to snore next to her, tucked up to the chin under silk sheets. Looking into his pampered, noble face, inside the echo of Rosewine Estate, she felt a deep-seated anger reignite. She imagined Crennel lying helpless in bed, his body falling limp before her. Without realizing it, she manifested a blade in front of her hand, the tip pointed at Lord Tulkarr, ready to shoot forward at a moment's notice.

She snapped back to her senses and dissipated the blade a second later. What was she thinking? A shiver ran through her body at the realization of what she had almost done. Before anything more could happen, she spun on her heel and sped out of the room. She closed the door behind her, her eyes catching the men lying on the floor, unable to avert her gaze any longer.

The blood had spread far past them and seeped into the carpet below. Their gurgles and whimpers had died off, their bodies frozen in their final moments. Her eyes fixed on the corpses and remorse gripped her heart. Regret and sadness swirled inside her mixed with anger at being forced to take their lives. Underneath it all, however, was a small spark of strength.

Leaving the manor was as easy as breaking in, thankfully, without any additional run-ins with Lord Tulkarr's staff. She jumped down from the tree and landed hard on her feet, though it was nothing compared to the pain that coursed through her body. Breathing still hurt; her stomach still threatened to lose its contents, and her mind raced with everything that had happened.

Serennia walked the streets of Ruddreth back to the Albatross, the pain from her break-in settling as a deep ache in her bones. She kept the two stolen rings in different pockets, each hand fidgeting with one of them, the busyness of her fingers helping to keep her mind distracted. The sight of the guards lying dead on the floor still burned behind her eyes, lurking, waiting to jump to the forefront the moment she let her guard down.

Something moved to her right. A figure, still hidden in the shadows, stood from one of the benches ahead and began to move towards her. She hesitated for a moment as she thought of running. But what would that accomplish? If they were after her, they'd give chase, and there was no way she was outrunning them in her current state. If it was a coincidence, she'd make herself look guilty, and that could attract the city watch.

She kept her chin up and approached the figure as it drew closer. Her heart raced faster with every step, her breaths coming more and more rapidly. When they were only a few feet away from each other, the figure—whose hooded cloak prevented her from making out their face—spoke.

"Did you succeed?"

She knew that voice. It took her a moment, but she was able to place it as Taza's. She should have known he wouldn't wait to check on her. The longer they waited to contact her, the more time she had to change her mind.

Serennia took the diamond ring out of her pocket and tossed it to Taza. He caught it with one hand, and in a fluid motion, placed it in his own pocket without stopping to inspect it.

"Well done. I'll be honest, I didn't think you would succeed. I suppose I should have known better than to question Genn's choices."

"Now what? Have I passed your test, or do you have more gruelling tasks to put me through?"

"Now, now, don't sound so upset. You accomplished your task; you should take pride in that." Serennia hated the way he spoke to her, as if she was a child that needed guidance. "As for what comes next, I'll need you to hang tight for now. I'll report to Genn the results of your mission, and he'll decide where we go from there."

Taza continued in the direction he had been heading. Serennia tried to ask him how long she would have to wait, but he acted as though he hadn't heard. More than a little frustrated, Serennia clenched her fists and convinced herself not to follow him. *I'd only be making things worse. As much as I would like to beat some answers out of him.*

Serennia let her anger evaporate into the night as she walked the rest of the way to the Albatross. It was late enough that only the rowdiest of patrons remained, so she let herself in the back door through the kitchen. It led out to a doorway right beside the stairs, and on the few occasions she had used it, she'd been able to cross the short distance without anybody noticing her.

Back in her room, with the moonlight casting longer shadows than usual and the winds whispering of her sins, she lay down and hoped that her dreams would offer her some reprieve.

Chapter 7

Everything felt wrong. Serennia had killed people. The guards would have killed her given the chance, so she knew fighting back had been the only way to save herself. Same with the guards at Rosewine. Yet she'd come so close to killing Lord Tulkarr, an innocent man, without noticing what she was doing. Then again, anyone who lived in such an opulent house with such violent people in their employ couldn't be truly innocent.

She needed to not think about it. She needed something, anything, to get the thoughts out of her mind. She had spent part of the morning practising with her new ring on the rooftop of the Albatross, learning to draw power from it instead of her own reserve. But doing so only reminded her of the night before, and it wasn't long before she had to stop lest the thoughts consumed her.

She thought a walk would clear her mind. She was halfway to the wharf, the salty air and warm sun like a comfortable blanket around her, when Taza fell into stride beside her.

"What do you want?" Serennia asked, her mood almost immediately ruined by his arrival.

"Is that any way to greet a friend?"

"I'll let you know next time I see one."

"Acquaintance then," Taza said, seemingly amused by her response. "In any case, it seems you've proven yourself. Follow me."

Serennia hated the effect Taza could have with just a few simple words. Despite not knowing where he would lead her, she followed him. He led her down the street, weaving between the masses of people with little effort. The two rounded a corner into a narrow alleyway that the sun could barely illuminate as it slowly approached its zenith. The alley fed into an even smaller passage framed by houses, so narrow that they had to turn sideways in order to fit.

"Where are you taking me?" Serennia wasn't sure why she hadn't split from him in the crowds when she'd had the chance.

"You'll see when we get there." The more Taza refused to give her answers, the more Serennia wanted to lash out. She hoped they would arrive wherever they were headed soon or she wasn't sure she could put up with Taza long enough to get there.

Several more twists and turns guided them around the backs of buildings until Serennia no longer knew where they were or how to get back to the main streets. They arrived at a dingy wooden door set into a derelict building. The wall around had no windows or signage, only plain brickwork matching the buildings around it. In the centre of the door were two triangles with their bases pressed against each other. It might have resembled a diamond if the bottom half wasn't twice the size of the top.

"We're here, Ren," Taza said.

"Don't call me that." Coming from him, the nickname felt like a knife in the gut. It reminded her too much of Lord Hauber and Cal and her parents. People that had loved her and done their best to make sure her life was as good as they could make it. Someone like Taza had no right.

He looked taken aback for a moment before making a quick recovery. "Well then, Serennia"—he placed extra emphasis on her name—"welcome to the Nest. Keep your head down, answer all questions honestly, and you'll be fine."

Taza opened the door, the slow *creak* bouncing off the walls around them and echoing down the alley. Beyond the threshold was a room small enough that Serennia could reach out and touch both sides with a staircase in the centre. Torchlight flickered from somewhere in the distance, casting the hallway in a soft orange glow that dissipated halfway from where she stood.

"Ladies first." Taza swept his arm forward, his head bowed with a slight smirk on his face. Serennia hesitated, but she knew she didn't have much of a choice. Who knew what the Sparrows would do if she refused them now that she had learned of their hideout.

She took a few cautious steps through the doorway and stopped at the top of the stairs. The bottom was beyond sight, somewhere past where the dim light faded into darkness.

"What's wrong? Afraid?" Taza stepped behind her and rested a hand on her back. Instinct kicked in and she shoved his hand off. "Feisty. I like it. You'll fit in well here." Taza winked and started down the stairs.

Not wanting to be left behind, Serennia followed him. The narrow steps forced her to watch where she placed each foot; it was hard not to trip. The stairs led to a wide, open room, illuminated by a multitude of different torches placed in sconces along the walls. People of all ages filled the room, some mingling with their comrades while others kept to themselves. A couple of young boys played a game of cards at a table in the centre.

When Taza and Serennia reached the bottom, they drew the attention of everyone in the room. A dozen sets of eyes all fixed themselves onto Serennia, studying the intruder in their home. She wished she could shrink into herself or fade into the shadows that played on the walls. Anything to get so many eyes off her.

"Who's she?"

"Did Taza get himself a girlfriend?"

"What is he thinking bringing a stranger down here?"

Questions murmured through the crowd, and Serennia noticed a few of them reaching for concealed weapons. Had Taza led her into a trap? Surely, they were just being cautious. She would have done the same. Still, she felt herself tensing up, prepared for a fight.

"Relax, guys, she's good. Genn's already approved her." Taza stepped in front of Serennia, one arm held out as if to protect her. The others slowly relaxed and returned to their prior occupations, though some kept a wary eye on her.

"I see you found our new recruit." A man stepped out from behind the two of them, his face somehow familiar. He looked to be at least twice Serennia's age, with ginger hair that had begun to grey around the edges. His eyes carried wisdom, the roughness of his skin speaking of a life that had been far from pampered, like he had been hardened beyond his years.

He stopped within an arm's length of Serennia and beckoned Taza away with a brief wave of his hand. The young man obeyed without question, leaving Serennia face to face with who she assumed was the leader of the Sparrows. The light cast long shadows on his angular face, highlighting the scar that extended from his temple and disappeared behind his stubble.

"It's nice to finally meet you, Genn." Serennia extended a hand in greeting, forcing herself to display a level of confidence that was foreign to her.

Genn looked down at her hand, then back up to her face. He gestured with his head towards a door in the back corner of the room. He didn't bother to wait for her to reply before he headed to it. Serennia followed him and he closed the door behind them, leaving them cut off from the rest of the Sparrows.

Inside, she found a room that ran counter to anything she could have expected. Shelves lined the walls, filled with tomes of all different sizes on a variety of topics. A desk sat at one end, similar to the one in Lord Hauber's study, covered in loose sheets of paper that partially covered a map of Ruddreth. Genn took a seat behind the desk and indicated for Serennia to take the spot opposite him.

He produced two goblets from somewhere beneath the desk, a matching pair with small, inlaid gemstones and gold accenting. He filled each with a measure of wine before sliding one of them to Serennia. Then he examined her for a moment, his eyes lingering on hers. She wanted to shrink and wished, not for the first time, that she wasn't so damn recognizable. Why couldn't she have been born with dark eyes like the rest of her people?

"I imagine you must have many questions." Genn spoke with a matter-of-factness, like conversations only existed to get a point across.

"What are the Sparrows?"

"Did Taza not tell you?"

"I want to hear it from you." She doubted he would say anything that would change her opinion, but it was as good a way as any to open up the conversation. Besides, even if he just reiterated the same message, the way he said it might give away something of his intentions.

"We live in a world where prosperity is predetermined. Where some people get to live lives of ease and luxury simply because their forefathers had a lucky break. Few people in this world owe their success to their own hard work and choices. I believe the quality of one's life should be dependent on them, not on those who came before. I think it's unfair that certain people have to suffer through no fault of their own.

"Unfortunately, the people who thrive on inherited success are the ones who shape society and ensure that the system continues to run in the same broken way. The Sparrows work to undermine that system in hopes that, one day, we might have the chance to replace it with a better one. If you have ever wanted a world where people like you and me can truly be comfortable, then the Sparrows are your best shot."

Genn took a sip from his drink, letting the silence stretch out between them, his words embedding themselves in Serennia's brain. She sipped her wine while she thought through her response and found the flavour disarmingly familiar. She'd tasted it before, with its downplayed sweetness and slight floral notes. While she hadn't seen the label on the bottle, she knew without a doubt it was Rosewine.

Had Genn done that on purpose to throw her off guard? Or was it simply what he had on hand? Serennia tried to think back to her initial meeting with Ralsin when she had shared her name. How loudly had she been speaking? Could Genn have overheard her?

These questions wouldn't get her anywhere. For the time being, she had to focus on the conversation at hand. She sat her cup down on the desk and drew a deep breath, her eyes never straying from Genn's.

"If I were to join you, what would you have me do?" Serennia still knew very little about the secretive inner workings of the Sparrows, and while she doubted they would do anything overtly malicious, she needed to make sure she at least had a rough idea of what she was getting herself into.

"Nothing you aren't comfortable with, I assure you. If you draw the line at thievery, then I will use you as nothing more than a pilferer. If, however, you are willing to do a wider variety of tasks, then I can guarantee there will be no shortage of work for you."

Serennia didn't know exactly what he meant by that, though she had some guesses. In truth, she wasn't sure where her line was these days. If she had been asked only a few weeks ago, she would have insisted that she'd never steal from anyone. But she'd done so much worse in the last couple of days. And she couldn't say she wouldn't do it again if given no other choice.

"So what do you say, Serennia? The Sparrows need all the help we can get, but as always, the choice is yours. I do not want you to feel pressured to join us."

This is it. The point of no return. Even with his supposed guarantee, she wasn't convinced she would be allowed to leave the Nest unscathed if she rejected Genn's offer. Yet as she sat at his desk, drinking wine that reminded her of her former home, she found that was less of a concern than she'd once thought.

"I'm in."

Chapter 8

Serennia prowled the streets of Ruddreth that had become like a second skin in the weeks since she'd proven herself to the Sparrows. What had once seemed like nothing more than a chaotic jumble was now a puzzle that she had solved. She had come to learn every turn, every building, and every dead end. She walked with confidence, weaving between crowds that barely noticed her passing, accompanied by one of her new cohorts.

As much as Serennia felt like she was beyond needing a minder, she couldn't have asked for a better companion. Harlee was only a couple of years older than her and was one of the friendlier members of the Sparrows. She kept the sides of her head shaved, the remainder of her chestnut hair pulled into a ponytail that reached almost to the base of her neck. Her muscular figure was hidden under a loose shirt and trousers, her well-developed forearms poking out from rolled up sleeves.

Genn had yet to send her on a mission that was anywhere near as harrowing as the first. When asked, he insisted on the importance of lying low as rumours of the Undying circled the city. Anything more than petty theft might draw their attention, and that could mean the end of the Sparrows.

Serennia and Harlee kept an eye out for potential threats as they walked the main thoroughfare. Genn hadn't given them an official task for the day, so Harlee suggested they find someone on which Serennia could refine her newfound skills as a thief. A stretch of poor weather had kept away the travelling merchants, so she was limited to tourists, roving mercenaries, and the like.

"That one," Harlee said with a minute tilt of her head. Serennia spotted a young man around their age walking towards them. His wallet was tied to his belt with no attempt at secrecy, his head looking around in the telltale fashion of a new arrival. His clothes didn't seem to indicate any notable wealth, but the fullness of his wallet suggested he had more than enough for what she needed.

Serennia walked towards her victim, surveying her surroundings while she kept him locked in her periphery. She had learned this from Taza—a foolproof way to rob just about anyone. All she needed were quick fingers and a convincing lie. It had yet to let her down. Harlee veered away, crossing to the other side of the street while Serennia closed in.

A minute later, she bumped into the man, hard enough to send them both tumbling to the ground. As they fell, she carefully slipped his wallet off his belt and onto her own with one hand, the other pressed against his chest to help knock him off balance. The impact was enough to force the air from her lungs, choking off any attempt at an exclamation.

"I'm so sorry!" Serennia was sure to speak loudly enough to hide any sound the wallet might have made. "I wasn't watching where I was going; I should have been paying more attention."

"H-hey, don't worry about it." The man tried to chuckle with what little breath he'd been able to regain. "I was a little distracted myself."

Serennia pushed herself back to her feet and brushed the dirt from her clothes. "I guess we'll both have to be more careful in the future." She walked away without another word, the young man still sprawled out on the ground behind her. The faster she left, the further away she'd be when he realized he was a couple of pounds lighter.

Within moments Serennia had disappeared around a corner and into the back alleys of Ruddreth. She heard vague sounds of alarm in the distance, though she knew she had nothing to worry about. The only people who knew the maze of alleys better than herself were on her side.

When the sound had faded to a dull murmur and rows of buildings surrounded her on all sides, Serennia removed the pouch from her belt. She counted the coins inside as she thought of all the ways she could spend it. The young man had been carrying a small fortune, more than she had seen in one place since she'd arrived. Had she robbed some noble's kid by mistake? She decided not to think too hard about it. Served him right if she had.

"Well done." Harlee appeared from around a corner, a smile lighting up her face. "You're starting to look like a professional."

"I learned from the best." Serennia reached into the wallet and passed a handful of coins to Harlee. Their agreement had been to split the earnings, though Serennia still walked away with a much larger share.

The pair stuck to the alleys until they were on the other side of town. Serennia didn't know if the boy would try to track her down, or what route he would take if he did, so she wasn't taking any chances. They made it to the northern end of the city and emerged back onto the main road, with Serennia glancing in every direction for her recent victim before she committed to walking out in the open.

Harlee parted not long after, likely to spend her day's earnings. Serennia worked her way towards the charity kitchen, eyes peeled for anyone who might have witnessed her crime. Thankfully, she doubted anyone other than the young man would be able to pick her out of the crowd. That was one of the biggest advantages of Ruddreth. While her darker skin and pale hair made her stand out in Alcress, Ruddreth was enough of a melting pot that she saw people who looked like her daily.

When she stepped through the door of the kitchen, Ralsin was quick to greet her with a smile and a friendly wave. Serennia had become familiar with all the volunteers, along with most of the patrons, though she didn't actually know most of the latter's names, referring to them with vague descriptions.

"We're going to be closing up for the afternoon soon, but there's enough left for you to have a bowl if you're hungry." Ralsin stirred his pot with one hand, and judging by the metallic scraping noise, it was almost empty.

Halfway through her bowl of soup, the door swung open to reveal a woman that looked to be nearing middle age with two young boys. The mother wore the same confused look Serennia had had on her first visit. They stepped up to the counter to receive their bowls of soup.

"I've never seen your face around here before," the worker said. She was a short, portly woman who had only recently started volunteering at the kitchen. Serennia was pretty sure her name was Venra, though she wasn't yet confident enough to use her name in direct conversation. "Are you new to Ruddreth?"

The mother hesitated a moment before she responded. "No, I grew up here. Just fell on some hard times and didn't have anywhere else to turn."

"I understand that better than most." Venra scooped a ladleful of soup into each of their three bowls, tilting the pot to get full scoops from what was left. The family stayed standing in front of the counter.

Tears began to leak out of the woman's eyes. "My husband was a guard at Lord Tulkarr's manor. He was killed in the break-in last month. He left us some money, but it's starting to run dry and I don't know what to do." By the end of her sentence, she was fully weeping.

The words hit like a hammer strike to Serennia's chest. The image of the dead soldiers burned in her mind, their final gasps and screams of pain echoing in her ears. Her spoon slipped out of her trembling hand and clattered against the bowl. The mother continued talking to Venra, but to Serennia it was little more than a dull roar in the distance.

She felt numb. It was like she had left her body, watching the scene play out from somewhere far away. Venra rounded the counter to wrap the woman in a hug and made sure to spare an embrace for each of the kids, who had started crying alongside their mother. Several of the patrons turned to watch the scene play out, though none of them moved to comfort the family.

Serennia's hands were in her lap, gripping each other so tightly that her nails broke skin. After a while, the family went to claim a table, and Serennia noticed she was staring. Did they know? Realistically, there was no way for them to have any idea that she had been the one who did it. Still, a thought latched into the back of her brain, whispering that they knew she was to blame; it was only a matter of time before they took their revenge.

Almost without thinking, Serennia rose from her seat, the last few spoonfuls of soup abandoned in the bottom of her bowl. Her feet shuffled, half-dragging across the wooden floor. When she drew near to the family's table, the mother looked up, which almost froze Serennia in her tracks. She pushed through with only a brief pause, so slight she hoped it went unnoticed.

"I heard what happened to you," Serennia said, unsure of what words to use. Were there any right words? "I'm so sorry for your loss." She cursed herself inwardly for the stupid, worn out phrase.

"Thank you. It's been difficult, but we're surviving." There was a hesitation in the mother's voice. Serennia felt she shouldn't have bothered them, that she shouldn't have intruded on this painful moment in their life.

"I'm sorry. I shouldn't be pestering you. I just wanted to give you this." Serennia pulled the stolen wallet off her belt and dropped it on the table. "I can only imagine the pain you're going through. I hope this helps."

Serennia took one step away from the table before the mother stopped her with a hand around the wrist. Serennia looked back over her shoulder to see that the woman had opened the wallet.

"We can't accept this. I appreciate the gesture, but this is too much."

"I insist. I don't need it."

The woman's eyes narrowed, suspicion growing within them. Oh Gods, had she somehow put it together? Did she know? "You're in a charity kitchen. What are you doing here if you're so rich you can just throw away a sum like this?"

Serennia searched for a lie that would calm suspicion. It didn't take her long to realize that the truth would be good enough. A version of it, anyway. "I just came into the money today. I stopped by the kitchen one last time because I've become friends with the workers, and I wanted to visit with them. But you need the money far more than I do. You've got kids to look after. I can survive on my own well enough."

The look of suspicion faded as Serennia spoke, replaced with a mist that grew into full tears by the time Serennia was done talking. An instant later, the woman threw her arms around Serennia's shoulders. Serennia didn't know what to do, her hands slowly reaching up to pat the woman on the back.

"Thank you so much. I wish more people were like you."

Serennia smiled in response, her mind completely devoid of words. When she was free of the woman's hold, she turned and left the kitchen behind. Any appetite she might have had was long gone, with no sign of coming back. The parting words stuck with her, replaying in her mind with each step through the alleyways. A part of her wanted to run back and tell the family the truth, to let them yell and berate her the way she deserved.

The world didn't need more people like her. It already had one, and that was too much.

Chapter 9

Serennia sat on the roof of the Albatross, watching as the clouds made their lazy journey across the sky. She wondered what it would be like to be so unrestrained, to go wherever the wind took her without a care. When she was a child, her parents had taken her to the beach. Though the memories were about as solid as the wispy clouds overhead, the parts she could remember filled her with a solemn joy. How different her life might have turned out, if not for the Arcanaeum.

She'd been sitting on the roof of the inn long enough that the minutes had melded into hours. After running into that poor mother, she had needed some time away from everything to process. Because of her, those boys didn't have a father. But if she hadn't done what she had, she wouldn't have survived. Was her life worth more than that of the three guards?

Footsteps sounded on the rooftop behind her. A spike of tension shot through every muscle in her body. Her brain raced with how she could strike them down before they drew too close. Only a couple of people knew about her penchant for spending time on the roof, and though she felt confident she could take any of them in a fight, there was no way to guarantee they were the culprit. They could have told someone, or she might have been followed. Had Crennel's people finally found her? Or the Undying?

Whoever it was continued their approach, though each step sounded drawn out. Serennia pushed off her feet and spun to face the intruder, her right arm extended in front of her, blades coalescing in front of her fist. She dropped into a crouch, wary of any potential shots aimed at her head. A silent curse echoed through her mind for standing so close to the edge. Even if she won the fight, it wouldn't take much for her to be sent to her death.

The intruder was a man that couldn't have been much older than herself. His black hair was cropped short, his eyes a deep shade of green. She'd seen those features before. It was the boy from that morning.

He stopped in his tracks, eyes fixated on her blades, though he seemed otherwise unaffected by the threat levelled at him. In one of his hands was a loaf of bread, a faint trail of steam rising from it. He held it out to her.

"I figured you were probably hungry. I thought maybe we could split it?" He seemed to briefly rethink his words. "Or you could have the whole thing to yourself if you'd rather."

"How did you find me?" She did her best to make sure her words warned of the violence she'd deliver if he tried anything.

"Ralsin, I think his name was? The man that works at the soup kitchen. He said you frequented the Albatross, and the innkeeper told me to check the roof. It was tricky getting up here without ruining the bread."

Serennia would have to remember to chastise Ralsin and Amira the next time she had the chance. There wasn't much point in having a secret spot if it was broadcast to anyone who asked about it. *Might have to scout out a new spot to relax if this one's going to bring me visitors.*

"Thank you," Serennia said, the words hollow and obligatory. She knew he would show his true colours before long; she could count on one hand the number of people that had been altruistic towards her.

She took the proffered food and felt its warmth radiate through her hand. Steam billowed from the inside as she tore a piece off, exposing the light and airy interior contained within the darkened crust. The first bite was better than most of what she'd eaten in Ruddreth.

The man still stood in front of her, a slight smile on his face. A lesson her father had taught her only months before his death echoed in her mind. *What we put into this world is what it will give back to us. Kindness is most important when it is difficult.* She'd stolen all this man's money, and instead of getting revenge, he'd brought her food. Serennia split the loaf in half and held the unbitten end out to him.

"You don't have to share if you don't want to. It's all yours, really." He held his hands in front of him, as if to protect himself from the bread.

"I can't eat it all myself." It was a lie, but she had a feeling insistence wouldn't get her far. "Besides, I know you don't have much money. I'd feel even worse if I took the only food you could afford." She was surprised to find that she was telling the truth about that part.

His smile widened as he accepted the offer. "Thanks, I appreciate it. And if it makes you feel better, you didn't get *that* much of my money. My mother always taught me to never keep more in my purse than I can afford to have stolen."

Serennia smiled despite herself. "I'm sorry. I know how hard it can be to survive in this city. I shouldn't have made things harder for you."

He waved away her concerns like they were a persistent fly. "Don't worry about it. If you stole it, I'm sure you must have really needed it."

At Serennia's invitation, they took a seat on the edge of the roof, the conversation replaced by silent stares at the burgeoning sunset. Serennia savoured the fresh food with each slow bite. She had no idea where he'd gotten the bread from, but she was certain it wasn't from anywhere in the outer city. The crust was perfectly crispy, and the dough hadn't been padded with crushed seeds to make up for using less flour.

"I'm Emrys." He spoke around a mouthful of food, crumbs clinging to the edges of his lips.

She didn't respond at first. She was still hesitant to let people know her name, though it hadn't brought her any harm yet. *Why is this so hard? Just tell him your damn name.* It was a stupid thing to have difficulty with, she knew. Eventually, she was able to force it out. "Serennia."

"You have really interesting eyes." Serennia almost choked on her bread. Did he know her secret? Was he a servant of the Arcanaeum who had finally tracked her down? Or maybe he had been hired by Crennel to kill her.

Emrys chuckled. "Wow, that came out a lot worse than it sounded in my head. I've just never seen a Garleshi without dark eyes before, certainly not as light as yours. They almost look like glass. I like them, though. They suit you."

What did she say to that? Did he want her to return the compliment? She wished she'd had more practice with these kinds of casual conversations.

"Did you grow up in Ruddreth? I could use someone who knows the area."

Serennia wasn't sure where she was from, really. Her parents had lived in a small cabin far from any of the major cities, near the southern border of Meldain. She had spent years living at Rosewine, enough that it also felt like home. "No, I didn't. I've only lived here for a month or so."

"Well you've got me beat. I just got here yesterday." Emrys had finished his dinner and stared out at the distant ocean. Serennia ate the last couple bites of her own food, a twinge of sadness panging in her heart at the thought of the delicious bread being gone.

"You'll pick it up in no time. The city looks chaotic and confusing, but you get used to it." She remembered when she had first arrived, when she'd thought the city was nothing more than twisting roads and dead ends. The

Sparrows had taught her the layout until it felt as natural to her as eating or breathing.

"Thanks, but I'm not sure I'll be here long enough for that."

"What are you, some kind of drifter?" Serennia had heard of people like that, who moved from one city to another, never putting down roots. A part of her envied them, though she did enjoy having a place that she could go back to at the end of the day.

"Yeah, something like that." The tone of his voice betrayed some other meaning.

"You're on the run, aren't you?"

"Is it that obvious?"

"Nah, just takes one to know one." While she hadn't had a run-in with the Undying since her parents' deaths, it didn't change the fact that the Arcanaeum would do anything to get their hands on her.

They had already sacked her home in an attempt to capture her, and much of her time in Ruddreth had been spent looking over her shoulder and jumping at shadows. Enough years had passed that they might not remember what she looked like, an idea that she clung to with whatever optimism she had. Maintaining her secret was the only thing keeping her safe from them, and she had almost given herself away only minutes ago when Emrys had snuck up on her.

"So you're a thief *and* a runaway? Sounds like an exciting life." Ordinarily Serennia would have lashed out at a comment like that. Something about the levity in his tone drew a sharp, humoured exhale from her instead.

"Not sure I would have chosen it, but I suppose it could be worse."

Emrys sighed and leaned back on his hands, his head tilted up to the sunset. "I know the feeling of being forced into a life you don't want. You just assume your parents know what's best for you, and by the time you realize they're wrong, it's too late to do anything about it."

Serennia didn't say anything. How could Emrys know how she felt? The terrors she'd been forced to endure, the horrors that had shaped her and forced her into the life she was now living. Nobody could know what that was like.

"I haven't seen my parents in years," Emrys continued. "I often wonder what they would think about the person I've become. They expected so much from me, and now here I am"—he gestured with one arm, a sweeping motion across the skyline before them—"running away from the life they wanted for me, doing things they wouldn't approve of. I love my parents. I really do. Still, a part of me can't help blaming them for how things turned out."

His voice grew small by the end. Serennia knew the sound of someone being choked by memories and wished there was something she could do to help. But how could she help someone else when she couldn't even help herself?

"I'm sure your parents only wanted what was best for you too," Emrys said, almost back to his normal volume.

"My parents weren't the problem," Serennia half snapped, then regretted her reaction. He wasn't trying to insinuate anything. He was just working with what little knowledge he had. She shouldn't have let her emotions get the better of her.

"I'm sorry," she said, noting the mild surprise on Emrys's face. "My parents were wonderful, but they were killed when I was young. My adoptive father did everything he could to care for me. He bought me gifts, spent time with me whenever he could, even taught me how to defend myself."

"How to defend yourself or how to fight?" Emrys asked, and she sensed some deeper meaning lurking beneath his words.

"What's the difference?"

"I had someone take me in once, and they said they would teach me how to defend myself. Before I knew it, I was a mercenary for their cause."

"Lord Hauber would never have used me like that. He was a good man."

"Sorry, I didn't mean to imply anything. I shouldn't make assumptions about people I've never met. I'm sure he was as great a person." Emrys turned his attention away from her once again, his gaze somewhere beyond the horizon.

She hated that their conversation had turned so confrontational. Had it been her fault? Was she too defensive? *It was nobody's fault.* They were just two people who had been through too much, and if he was anything like her, those experiences coloured every interaction he had.

Silence enveloped them once again as the vibrancy faded from the evening sky. Despite the emotion that saturated the end of their exchange, it was a more comfortable silence than Serennia was used to. She didn't feel the need to fill it with pointless small talk or leave to escape its crushing weight. For once she was content to just exist in the moment, her thoughts temporarily free of haunting reminders, watching as the sun sank below the horizon somewhere far beyond the ocean.

"I should probably get going." Emrys stood up and brushed the dust from his backside. He took a couple of steps away from the edge, which prompted Serennia to stand up as well. He turned to face her and held out one hand. "It was nice meeting you, Ren."

Any words Serennia had been about to say arrested in her throat. She only allowed those closest to her to call her that, so why didn't she hate it coming from Emrys? He had been kind to her after what she'd done, so maybe he had earned the right.

"It was nice meeting you too, Em." She hesitated for a moment. "How long are you in Ruddreth for? We could meet again if you'd like. I promise I won't rob you this time."

Emrys laughed. "I appreciate it, but I'm leaving tomorrow. You're welcome to see me off at the docks though."

Serennia took Emrys's outstretched hand in hers, clasping it perhaps a little tighter than she should have.

She wasn't sure what else to do. "Thank you again for the food. I'll do my best to see you tomorrow, but just in case I don't, I hope you have a safe trip."

The two shook hands, and Emrys offered her a warm smile. "It was my pleasure. I hope to see you tomorrow, Ren." He crossed back to the far side of the roof, where Serennia noticed the ladder he had propped up. He swung one foot onto the top rung, then paused and looked at her one last time. "You might want to keep that magic under wraps. The Undying are patrolling the area." He disappeared down the ladder.

As she watched him go, Serennia swore to herself she would repay him somehow, no matter how long it took. For starters, she would head down to the wharf and see him off. Maybe she could bring him a gift of some kind as a thank you for the bread. After he'd been so kind to her, she figured it was the least she could do.

Chapter 10

The sun shone high above the main streets of Rud-dreth, illuminating the cobblestone streets of the inner city. Tall buildings framed the path, transitioning to shorter, squatter buildings as the bay drew closer, the houses and shops replaced with warehouses and open markets. Serennia strolled towards the wharf, a fresh loaf of bread under one arm. It had cost most of the money she'd saved up, yet she didn't mind.

Harlee had tagged along, expecting an afternoon of robbing unsuspecting victims. It had taken some time for Serennia to convince her that it was just an ordinary visit to the docks, and she was amazed that Harlee had still agreed to come, albeit with minor protesting.

The sound of commotion drew Serennia's attention. One of the Undying—a knight of the Arcanaeum in full, slate-grey plate armour—strode down the street like it belonged to them, flanked by a squire on either side. The two up-and-coming Undyings wore only cuirasses and chain mail, sheathed longswords hanging loosely from their belts. The knight carried no weapon that Serennia could see.

A mix of instinct and fear spurred Serennia's legs into action, propelling her into a run in the opposite direction. Harlee shouted after her, though the words didn't register. Her first couple of steps sent her straight into another squire, her head colliding with his chest. She looked up to find nothing but steely determination on his face.

"Running from the Undying, are we?" His voice was full of haughty pomp, and she couldn't tell if he was born noble or just trying to sound important. "Your reaction betrays your guilt. Come with me and—" His words froze as the two of them made eye contact. She tried to look away, but it was already too late. Her eyes had given her away.

Serennia broke into a full sprint away from the squire, narrowly avoiding his attempt to grab her. She had dropped the bread when she bumped into the man, and a part of her cursed for wasting it. But she couldn't worry about that. If those squires caught her, nothing good awaited. Her life depended on losing them among the twists and turns of the streets.

Shouts echoed from behind as she tore into the alleys. Seconds later, arcane energy shot past her head and collided into the wall in front of her. Chips of stone and dust flew into the air. She had a vague awareness of the man yelling for her to stop, the words lost in the distance.

She turned a corner and came to a halt a few steps down the alleyway. Two blades materialized above her arm, aimed straight ahead. It was the only way she stood a chance of escape. Even though she knew the streets better, he was faster, and with him firing missiles at her, her chances of getting away unscathed were next to nothing. If she couldn't flee, then once again she was left with no other choice.

The moment she saw the beginning of the man's body, she fired. One blade missed, the other sliced deep across his thigh. She didn't wait to watch him drop. Her feet pounded the cobbles as she heard him stumbling to the ground.

Her breath came in ragged bursts, but she couldn't allow herself to stop. She knew reinforcements were on their way; she could hear the distant sound of footsteps accompanied by shouts drawing closer. Her chest burned with each step, her lungs on fire as they strained to keep up. She only needed to make it a little further. The Albatross was a few streets away; then she could hole up in her room until everything blew over.

One more turn brought her face to face with her worst nightmare. A knight of the Undying stood in the middle of her path, sword drawn, sunlight reflecting off armour that was such a dark purple it appeared black. The only parts of their body not covered in plate armour were beneath chain mail, leaving no obvious weak spot. The signature mask of the Undying covered their face, an emotionless visage that revealed only the eyes.

"So this is where you've been hiding." The knight's voice rumbled out of him. "You'd be wise not to make this a fight. I would much rather bring you in alive and of your own volition."

"I sincerely doubt that." Memories of her childhood stormed through Serennia's mind. The last time she had seen one of those masks it had been in the doorway of her childhood home, her parents standing between it and her. Moments before she was forced to run, abandoning the only home she'd ever known, never to see her parents again.

"You should consider yourself fortunate. Had we realised that you were the one he was after you might have ended up with far worse than me on your trail. I'm more lenient than many of my cohorts. Perhaps that Brathis fool didn't know what was living under his roof."

Two squires came running down the alley and stopped behind Serennia. Her heart beat so hard she thought it might break through her chest. Should she surrender and let them take her? That would be easier than inviting whatever he planned if she fought back.

No. The Arcanaeum would make her into their own personal weapon, even if they had to break her to do it.

Serennia summoned blades on either side of her body. She heard the squires shuffle their feet behind her, probably dropping into battle stances. The knight laughed, the sound rumbling out from behind his mask like distant thunder.

"Go assist the others," he said, gesturing slightly to one side with his head. "I'll take care of this one." The squires paused for a second before obeying, taking off the way they had come.

"I may have orders not to kill you, but that still leaves me with plenty of options to make you regret raising your hand against me."

Her exit wasn't blocked anymore, though running would be just as dangerous as fighting. He may have had orders not to kill her, but she didn't plan on giving him any other option. She'd rather die than be delivered into the hands of the Arcanaeum.

Serennia's conjured blades shot forward, slicing through the air towards the knight. The edge of his sword came alive with arcane energy, the blade swinging around to deftly block each of her attacks.

"Is that all?" He took a couple of slow steps in her direction, the tip of his weapon dragging along the ground. "My turn."

The knight swung his sword at Serennia's chest; she almost fell backwards as she dodged. She threw more blades at him. He deflected each one without any apparent effort. More wide slashes pushed her back, some closer than others, the arcane edge digging deep grooves through the stone of the buildings on either side of them.

As the adrenalin in her system spiked, images came flooding back to her. The Undying breaking down the door of her home. Blades drawn on all sides as her parents fought desperately to protect her. Her mother's screaming face, urging her to run.

The Undying were to blame for everything that had happened to her since. Weeks spent living in the wilderness, years under Crennel Brathis. Because she was powerful, and they wanted that power for themselves.

Rage built like a wildfire in her chest. If they wanted her power, she'd be happy to give them a taste. Blades sprang into being around her, one after another, until over a dozen of them floated around her head. Pain surged through her body, growing with each new weapon she spawned. She should have pulled from the ring, rather than take such a toll on her body. At that moment, she didn't care.

With a single push, she threw them all at her opponent, more than he could ever hope to parry, though she knew hc would try. The knight backstepped as he swung his sword around to block. While most of the blades died against his weapon, a few made it past his defences. Most of them only gouged his armour, though one managed to draw blood across his sword arm.

"Well, well, look who's learning to fight back," the knight taunted. "This would have been so much easier if you'd seen reason. Then again, your futile resistance is more fun."

Serennia could hear the knight's smirk in his voice. It only made her angrier. If he expected an easy fight from her, she'd make sure to prove him wrong.

She continued to dodge his attacks the best she could, throwing her own at him whenever she saw an opening. One of his swings sliced across her midsection, the arcane energy burning as the steel slid through her skin. It was only a shallow wound, which was good, because she had no time to worry about it.

Another swing came at her head. She leaned back, allowing the blade to pass inches from her face. The knight took advantage of her poor stance and drove a kick into her stomach, exactly where the blade had already cut her. Pain burst through her body as she stumbled backwards, only barely able to keep her balance by gripping a nearby wall.

He lunged again, swinging for her outstretched hand. The blade smashed into the brick as her arm withdrew, but his attack brought him in close enough to land a violent backhand across her face. His armoured glove *cracked* against her jawline and she saw stars.

She didn't know how long they'd been fighting. Time stretched on, and she had yet to land another meaningful hit against him. She needed to end the fight. The longer she delayed, the worse her chances got. Serennia launched another handful of blades at the knight and managed to land a hit against his leg, the energy stabbing through the chain mail as if it were clothing and penetrating out the other side. The knight was able to stay upright, though she heard an audible grunt of pain from behind the mask.

She had her opening.

Every ounce of energy in her body went into her next attack. Arcane blades coalesced not only around her, but around the knight. She lost count of how many spikes she'd conjured, filling the space between them, until the pain felt like it would rip her body apart. Her breath grew heavy, the light in her stolen focus ring dimming as the agony forced her to draw beyond her own power.

Serennia's right hand was level with her head, her fingers curled into a claw as she struggled to fight through the torture. The knight looked at her, and through the eyeholes in his mask, she saw what she hoped was fear. All the blades converged on their target at once. Any attempts at defence the knight made were weakened by his injured leg; he was incapable of preventing the brunt of the storm that rained down on him.

When all the energy had dispersed, the knight was left with deep scars across his armour. Blood seeped from multiple wounds, his body sagged, and his sword clattered to the ground. The knight dropped first to his knees, then fell face first to the ground. Blood spread out from his body as his last breaths came out in sputtered coughs.

It took a while for Serennia's brain to process what had just happened. The Arcanaeum had come for her, and she had stopped them. She looked at her hands, which shook from exertion. She'd killed someone again. Why was it that she seemed unable to avoid taking lives? Somehow, though, this one wasn't clawing its way into her brain like the last one. She looked at the newly made corpse, blood pooling beneath it, and her eyes didn't beg to turn away.

In that moment, she felt unstoppable.

Chapter 11

The corpse was still slumped behind a stack of crates when Serennia returned to the alleyway. She was relieved it hadn't been moved. With any luck, that meant it hadn't been spotted either. A corpse was a common enough occurrence in the slums of Ruddreth, but the corpse of an Undying would cause unmitigated panic. Per their name, the knights were said to be immortal, sent by the Five to enforce their divine will. If the Arcanaeum got word that one of their elites was lying dead in the outer city, Serennia doubted even the King would be able to stave off their reprisal.

She'd spent the better part of the last hour trying to figure out how to dispose of the body. For every idea she thought of, there were too many reasons it would never work. Then it hit her. She didn't have to hide the body at all. She just had to hide the fact that it belonged to one of the Undying.

The armour was tricky to remove; some of the segments locked together. Eventually, she got every piece off and separated. She placed them all into a large burlap sack she had purchased from a merchant at the other end of the slums. There were likely closer merchants she could have purchased from, but she was being cautious.

When she removed the helmet and mask—which seemed to have somehow fused together—she hesitated. Something felt wrong. She had to fight the urge to toss it away and be rid of it. A look inside revealed arcane symbols carved into the metal of the mask, each giving off an impression of malice. She tucked it into the sack, which filled it almost to bursting, and tied off the end as tightly as she could manage.

With her baggage in tow, Serennia walked the short distance to the back entrance of the Albatross. She snuck past the kitchen staff while their backs were turned, peeking through a crack in the door to the main room before she crept through. She made sure to close the door as quietly as possible so as not to attract unwanted attention.

Keeping the sack of metal from making noise was difficult; the various plates clinked together with every step she took. She held the armour in one arm, the other hand in a tight grip around the top to keep it from coming undone. She trudged up the staircase with slow, precise steps, careful not to do anything that might turn heads in her direction. Her pace quickened when she reached the second-floor hallway, hurrying to reach her door before anyone poked their head out of their room. She threw the door open, used her back to push it closed behind her, and dropped her acquisition to the ground.

It took a few moments for Serennia to catch her breath and calm the thunder in her chest. When the excitement had passed, she knelt down in front of the trunk that sat at the foot of her bed and examined the lock. For a moment, she considered asking Amira for the key, but she realized that might raise suspicions. It wasn't a conversation she was confident she could navigate without incriminating herself.

With a careful focusing of magic, she was able to extend a blade from two outstretched fingers that sliced clean through the lock. The bottom half clattered to the ground, the loop on top still hooked through the latch. She slid the scrap of metal out and tossed it aside unceremoniously before flipping open the lid.

Rather than the empty trunk she had expected, a stack of papers was spread across the bottom. She reached down and scooped them up. A quick scan revealed that much of it was nonsense, at least as far as she was concerned. They made brief mentions of something called the Broken Rose, which appeared several times throughout the letters and schematics.

One page seized her attention. A list of names and professions, with their locations listed beside each one, as well as what she assumed to be some kind of indication of their allegiance. She found Lord Hauber, Ralsin, and Amira among the names, each one with "Trusted" written next to it.

"What is this?" Serennia muttered.

A closer look through the names revealed Telbek and Imra with the same denotation. She didn't recognize any of the others, yet it made her wonder how far the web spread. The list contained names from all over the continent, even some she suspected were in other parts of the world.

What kind of organization had Lord Hauber been a part of? Who were all these people? All the names she recognized were people who had helped her in some capacity. Was it all coordinated somehow? Or had it been mere chance that brought her to them?

Serennia remembered what Emrys had told her about people taking him in and using him for their ulterior motives. *No. Lord Hauber was better than that.* She refused to believe that she had been anything more than a daughter to him.

Thinking of Emrys only made her angrier. She had been so close to finally having someone she could consider a friend, but the Arcanaeum had stolen that from her, too. Had those Undying not pursued her, she could have met with him at the pier, maybe even gone with him to somewhere safer. By the time she'd escaped, his ship had already set sail.

She replaced the papers in the trunk and set the bag of armour on top. Whatever else those papers contained, she couldn't think about it for the time being. She had to find a way to safely dispose of the armour that wouldn't lead back to her. Then she could search for answers.

* * * * *

Serennia pushed open the door to the charity kitchen, walking past the stack of bowls by the entrance, her vision locked on Ralsin behind the serving counter. It was early afternoon, which meant the building would be closing soon. A few patrons sat on their own, spaced throughout the dining room, while the servers chatted amongst themselves.

"Is everything alright, Serennia?" Ralsin asked as she approached the counter.

"I need to talk to you about something." She made a conscious effort to dull her words, reminding herself that Ralsin wasn't at fault for whatever she discovered.

"What's on your mind?" He seemed unnerved, though she supposed she couldn't blame him.

Serennia drew in close, unsure what kind of reaction she would get from the other volunteers if they heard what she was about to say. "What is the Broken Rose?"

Ralsin smiled. "You mustn't say that name so openly." His voice was so quiet she could barely hear him.

He straightened, then turned to the side with a hand out to forestall any further words from Serennia. "Venra, would you mind covering me for a few minutes? Serennia and I need to discuss something in private."

"As long as you're back by the dinner rush," Venra said.

"I'd be worried if I was gone anywhere near that long," Ralsin joked. Then he gestured for Serennia to round the counter and led her through a door into the backroom of the kitchen.

While the main room smelled like a delicious meal, this room smelled like its infancy. Shelving lined the wall, filled with various vegetables and spices. Serennia could pick out the scent of almost every one, though the smells hit her individually, overlapping and fighting with one another, rather than mingling together to form that of a hearty stew. In the corner, a large cauldron sat above coals and ash, and she figured that must be where they prepared the meals before partitioning them into the pots along the counter.

Ralsin grabbed one of the sets of shelves and pulled it away from the wall. She braced herself for an awful scraping sound, but it glided across the floor almost without a sound. Serennia peeked behind it and saw an old wooden trapdoor flush with the wall. Ralsin unlocked it with a key he produced from his pocket, revealing a staircase reminiscent of the one that led to the Nest.

Unlike the entrance to the Nest, this passage was lit by glowstones, their steady, clear light reaching further than that of torches. Seeing something so expensive hiding in a tunnel within a city like Ruddreth threw her off balance. Ralsin went in first, leaving Serennia to follow him into the underbelly of the city.

"Where are you taking me?" she asked after a time, hoping to break the tense silence.

"Somewhere private. The conversation you want to have is a dangerous one. I need to make absolutely certain that we cannot be overheard."

Serennia swallowed the lump that had formed in her throat. *What was Lord Hauber part of? Maybe he wasn't the paragon of kindness I thought he was*, a tiny voice in the back of her head nagged. She smothered that voice. Lord Hauber *had* been a good man. She was sure of it.

Soon they reached the bottom. The tunnel opened into a large, circular room that was at least double the size of the Nest. A stone table dominated the centre, wide enough that Serennia thought she could lie across the top without reaching the edge. Wooden chairs were pushed in around the circumference, several of them sporting thin layers of dust.

Ralsin crossed the room to the table, where he pulled out a chair and sat down. Serennia did the same, in part because it felt expected of her, and in part because she didn't know what else to do.

"Where did you hear that name?" Any trace of Ralsin's previous joviality was gone. In the light of the glowstones along the wall, the shadows on his face made him look almost like a different person.

"Lord Hauber left some notes about them in his old room." Serennia had debated whether she should tell Ralsin the truth about her information. In the end, she'd decided she would be better off risking the truth than her lies getting her into more trouble than she was already in.

Ralsin sighed and closed his eyes for a moment, one hand coming up to pinch the bridge of his nose. "Old Hauber always did have a habit of being a touch too...cavalier about these sorts of things. Tell me what you know."

Best to tread carefully, she knew. "I have a list of names for starters."

"So that's how you knew to approach me."

"You seemed like my safest bet." Ralsin only nodded in response, so Serennia continued. "I also have a medley of correspondence, among other things. I'd be happy to give them back to you, but only if you answer my questions."

Ralsin sighed and leaned back in his chair. "The Broken Rose is many things. The organization as a whole spans the continent, though most of the branches act largely independently from each other, united by the singular goal of reducing the Arcanaeum's influence on the world.

"The Ruddran branch often worked to undermine the nobility. We believed that by bolstering the lower class, they would be encouraged to rise up and fight for themselves. We thought it was better to bring the lower class up, rather than bringing the upper class down."

"You talk about it like it doesn't exist anymore."

"It might as well not." Ralsin slumped down, his eyes casting to his lap for a moment before returning to Serennia. "This branch of the Broken Rose was funded largely by Rosewine Estate, a resource we have lost. Many of our operations have been forced to cease, and others are slowly on their way out. Even the charity kitchen won't be able to last much longer."

"So Rosewine was a front for funding the Broken Rose?" Serennia realized the manor's name might have had a different meaning than she assumed. Lord Hauber had told her it was named after the Holy Rose of the

Pentad, but she saw now it had a clever—if thinly veiled—double meaning.

"More or less. Now that Crennel is in charge, our funding is all but nonexistent. We have reached out to him on numerous occasions, though each has been met with a more terse denial than the last."

Serennia clenched her fists until her knuckles turned white. One more thing that Crennel had ruined. His selfishness was no surprise, though she had hoped that even he would see the good that a group like the Broken Rose could do. It would explain where he'd got the money for all the additional guardsmen he had hired after Lord Hauber's death. She didn't know how much money Lord Hauber had given to the Broken Rose, but it sounded like a small fortune.

"Does that answer satisfy you? Or was there more you wanted to know?"

This was it. She had to ask the question that she'd been trying to ignore, the one that Emrys had planted in her brain and the letters had fuelled. "Did Lord Hauber ever talk about me to the rest of the Broken Rose?"

"All the time. He was so proud of you, always bragging to the other members whenever he had the chance. He thought you were capable of great things."

"As his daughter or as a weapon?"

"I do believe that he truly loved you as a daughter. There were times when he spoke of you only as his child, and he did so with a smile on his face. That may not have been his primary goal in raising you, but I think it became just as important by the end."

"I'd like to think that's true." It had to be. If it wasn't, then what else did she have? For so long, Lord Hauber's kindness had been the only light in her life. If she accepted that he'd had ulterior motives in raising her, she had nothing left to hold on to. He *had* loved her. She *was* his daughter, and that was all that mattered.

"Thank you," Serennia said, then rose from her chair. "I'll bring the letters by after dinner when the rush dies down."

"Keep them. I have no use for them anymore. Besides, the list of names may come in handy one day. While the Ruddran branch of the Broken Rose may be all but defunct, most of the others are still going strong. I'd be surprised if they weren't willing to help you if you called on them."

Serennia nodded. She had no words left. The voice in the back of her head was growing stronger. She needed to get out of this stone chamber, into the fresh air where she could smother the voices with a hundred different distractions.

Lord Hauber was a good person. She was his daughter and nothing else. Everything he'd ever done for her was for her own good, to make her life the best it could be.

She wouldn't allow the truth to be anything else.

Chapter 12

It never ceased to amaze Serennia how quickly alcohol could forge friendships. When she had first joined the Sparrows, the members were distant at best, often looking at her through glowers and stares that could pierce stone. After the first couple weeks, when she finally let her guard down and shared a drink with a few of them, that distance shrank rapidly. While some still preferred to keep to themselves, she now could call most of the Sparrows friends.

She sat with three of them around a table playing a game they called Beggar in the Alley, though it had been taught to her as Gods' Favour during her childhood in Rosewine. She was in the middle of a monumental losing streak, much to the entertainment of the other players. She attributed most of that to them playing by different rules, an opinion that had got her teased for "playing like a highborn" when she first brought it up. So she resolved to learn the "poor rules," as her friends so eloquently referred to them, while taking her mounting losses with a half-drunken grace.

Drinks flowed easily in the Nest in just about any variety one could imagine. They even had a few top-quality liquors in their inventory, though there was an unspoken agreement that those were saved for special occasions. Serennia often helped herself to the wine, since, having grown up in a winery, it was the only alcohol she could claim any familiarity with. Most of the Sparrows avoided it in favour of rum, which was fine by her. She liked not having to share.

"And to the surprise of no one," Harlee said as she threw down the card that declared her the winner, "Serennia loses again."

Luthe tossed his cards down on the table with an exasperated sigh. "One more round and I would have had it. My luck is ash." Until she had gotten to know him, Luthe had always come off as intimidating. He towered over almost everyone else in the room, his keen eyes always appraising, his sharp jawline accented by the beard he kept in a tapered point.

"Yeah, and a couple more coins would make me a noble." Mouse was one of the few people Serennia had encountered where you got exactly what you expected. His moniker stemmed from his stature, though his diminutiveness was offset by a level of energy that could be either infectious or tiring, depending on your mood. He kept his dirty blonde hair pulled back in a tail—which didn't help the nickname—and many of the strands had fallen loose over the course of their game.

Serennia drowned her laughter in her glass, the wine flowing smoothly across her tongue. It felt good to relax. How long had it been since she had felt so at ease?

Since before Lord Hauber's death, surely. Thinking of him brought questions to mind, ones that she was in no mood to try to answer. Instead, she smothered them in more drink.

"You up for another round, Serennia?" Harlee asked.

Before Serennia could answer, Taza stepped behind her and interjected. "Apologies, but I'm afraid you'll have to play this round without her. The boss has requested her presence."

His words brought a touch of sobriety to Serennia's addled mind. Her head swam as she stood, her steps uncertain, yet her thoughts sharpened in an instant. What could Genn want with her?

Taza led her across the room, their passage drawing the eyes of everyone as they walked by. It was well known among the Sparrows that Genn reserved personal audiences for jobs of great importance. That or punishments. Serennia wasn't sure which it would be, though she couldn't think of anything she might have done to warrant the latter.

When they reached the door at the far end of the room, Taza held it open for Serennia, then closed it behind her, remaining outside. She was alone with Genn in his makeshift office for the first time since she'd been given her initiation task.

"Serennia, please, have a seat." As he spoke, Genn produced a bottle of Rosewine from beneath his desk and poured her a glass. "I hear you favour wine. I'm sure you'd appreciate something better than the swill we keep out there."

She accepted the glass with a nod and a thanks, taking a sip so he'd know her appreciation was genuine. It was like comparing a days old, mealy apple to one fresh from the branch. If the other wine was a warming touch, this one was a loving embrace. The flavour danced through her mouth, free from the bitterness that tainted lesser vintages.

"I have an important job for you." Genn got straight to business, one hand idly swirling his own glass, filled with an amber liquor of some sort. "One that I'm not confident I can entrust to any of the others."

What's that supposed to mean? Serennia had only been a Sparrow for a little over a month, so there was no way she was already one of Genn's elites. There had to have been other members more capable of the job than she was.

"Does the name Lord Muretian sound at all familiar to you?" Genn asked, taking a sip from his drink.

"I'm afraid not, sir."

"As it shouldn't. He's a despicable man, one which you should count yourself lucky to have never crossed paths with. He was a soldier of much renown here in Ruddreth, enough to earn him the hand of Lady Muretian a few years back. Just a couple months ago, she died under questionable circumstances, leaving him the sole heir to her estate.

"Since then, he has been a stellar example of someone undeserving of their station." Genn pulled a folded page out of the inside of his jacket and slid it across the table.

Serennia unfolded the paper and began to read through its contents. It appeared to be a letter from some of his staff, detailing his various abuses against them. Verbal harassment, withholding pay over insignificant mistakes, public beatings. The list only continued to get worse; she was physically sick by the end. This man made Crennel look downright tolerable.

"I have some contacts within his staff who have compiled this list through personal sufferings and eyewitness accounts. They sought our help, and as such, we have brokered an agreement. In exchange for dealing with their problem, we're allowed to help ourselves to any riches within his manor."

"And you want me to...deal with their problem?" Serennia had a lurking feeling in her gut about what he was implying. She hoped it was wrong, but the realistic side of her knew she wasn't.

"Lord Muretian may be a fool on a stolen pedestal, but he is a hardened fighter. Any of the other Sparrows would be at a disadvantage if the job were to lead to an engagement. You, on the other hand, took out three of Lord Tulkarr's guards single handedly. Few of the others would be capable of success against such odds."

The arcane ring felt heavy in her pocket. She tried not to wear it openly, saving it for occasions where she thought she might need it. Genn couldn't know she had it, yet he was willing to risk this whole mission on her supposed combat skills. He didn't even have proof that she had been the one to kill those guards. Though given the circumstances, she was the most likely candidate.

"I don't know that I can accept this job, sir. I apologize, but I don't want to kill anyone." *Not again.* She let the words go unspoken.

"Tell me, Serennia. Are you familiar with the concept of the Cosmic Scale?" Genn's sudden change of topic caught Serennia off guard.

"Only vaguely. I've heard a few people mention it, but they never went into specifics and I never asked."

Genn gave her a slow nod, punctuated by a sip from his drink. Only when his drink was back on the desk did he continue. "It was proposed by a man named Gahtriel, who was one of the first major opponents of the Pentad. He believed that rather than their teachings of living free from conceived sin, and working to repent for sins committed, that our good deeds are weighed against the bad. Whichever one outweighs the other will determine the fate of our eternal souls—if you find yourself believing in such things."

"So followers can just perform evil deeds as long as they do enough good to counter them?" The whole system seemed a little convenient. If wrongdoings could be so easily nullified, what was the point of living a good life?

"I suppose you could boil it down that way, but the church's acolytes would argue that it is far more nuanced than that. It is not just the overall comparison of your life's choices. Each singular action must be weighed to determine whether it will be seen as a good deed or a bad one."

Serennia took another sip from her wine as the dots connected in her mind. "I suppose this is your way of telling me that killing Lord Muretian will be a good thing?"

"You catch on quickly." Something about Genn's smile was both rewarding and off-putting in equal measure. "You yourself saw the list of Lord Muretian's crimes. Can you deny that ridding the world of someone such as him would be a positive thing?"

"No, I can't."

"Lord Muretian keeps about twenty people on his staff. Sixteen of them contributed to this hit against him. Those that didn't corroborate the stories didn't defend him; they merely stayed silent out of fear of reprisal. He is a stain on this world and killing him can only make the world a better place."

Genn rose out of his chair, circling the desk to stand next to Serennia. "Killing is not an inherently evil act. If a prized horse has a parasite, do we curse the doctor for killing the parasite? It is a living creature, and yet its death is celebrated. Sometimes death is necessary, Serennia. People like Lord Muretian are the dying branches that must be pruned lest they bring the rest of the tree down with them."

Serennia looked up to where Genn stood beside her. She expected to find malice in his eyes or at least some anger. Instead, she found an overwhelming calmness plastered across his face. She realized he meant every word he said. He truly believed that death was a necessity, that the world would be a better place if people like Lord Muretian were simply killed.

Looking deep inside herself, Serennia found she agreed. How much better would her life and those of the employees of Rosewine be if Crennel had died? She took a deep breath and finished her wine, allowing the alcohol to quiet the ever-shrinking voice inside her that warned against her actions.

Chapter 13

Muretian's manor was smaller than Serennia had expected, though she supposed that was a good thing. The more expansive it was, the longer it would take to navigate, and the more chances there were for her and her team to get caught. Then again, it didn't seem like that would be a problem tonight. She had run into a few members of the staff within the couple of minutes she'd been inside, and they had pretended not to notice her. Serennia couldn't shake the feeling that this job was too easy. She shouldn't have been able to stroll through the manor as brazenly as she was.

Luthe, Mouse, and Harlee had accompanied Serennia, the three of them breaking away from her the moment they entered the foyer to pilfer goods to bring back to the Nest. She alone was responsible for taking care of the main job. No point exposing them to the danger if she didn't have to. At least, that was the reason she had given them. In truth, she didn't want them knowing what she was capable of. Better to let them think of her as a gifted fighter.

As Serennia turned down the hallway, she spotted a set of wooden double doors dominating the far wall. They were carved with various types of birds, some in flight while others rested on branches, alluding to Muretian's reputation as an avid birdwatcher. A single butler stood to the side of the door, presumably waiting for his name to be yelled from the room beyond. The man locked eyes with her and said nothing, offering only a single, shallow nod. He knew why she'd come. He'd likely helped to arrange it.

One last deep breath and Serennia crossed the remainder of the hallway. Her hands came to rest against the textured wood of the doors, arms preparing to throw them open. She spared one last look at the butler, at his reluctance to meet her eyes. She wanted to console him and wondered if there was anything she could say or do that might ease whatever burden was weighing on his mind.

"You're doing the right thing." It wasn't much, and the butler appeared not to have heard her. She supposed if the situation were reversed, she wouldn't have found much consolation in an assassin agreeing with her either. Oh well. Not much else she could do.

The doors were heavier than they looked; Serennia had to put most of her weight against them to make them move. They glided open with almost no sound, revealing a plush bedroom beyond. A four-poster bed sat at the far end, with ornate tables on either side. Paintings hung over every inch of wall. An expensive-looking rug covered much of the floor, and the dressers held what she was sure were prized sculptures. Even the windows were stained glass, bathing the room in multi-coloured hues.

Lord Muretian was fast asleep in his bed. Light footsteps brought Serennia across the room, one hand coming up to prepare for her attack. Slivers of magic coalesced above the bed, pointing down towards the lump under the blankets, ready to drop at a moment's notice.

Something was off. She studied the shape beneath the blankets, looking for anything wrong, anything that might explain the sinking feeling in her gut. *Am I just being overly cautious?* No, this was more than just anxiety.

He wasn't breathing.

Serennia stepped back and turned to survey the room just as the *twang* of a crossbow preceded a sharp pain across her arm. She threw herself over the bed in a roll, landing in a crouch on the other side, her hand instinctively going to the fresh wound. It didn't seem to be serious, thankfully. Just deep enough to draw blood that now stained her sleeve.

"I knew you'd come eventually," a voice called out from the other side of the room. "When I heard about the incident at Tulkarr Manor I knew it was only a matter of time before the intruders turned their sights on the star of the Ruddran army."

Serennia couldn't help rolling her eyes. *What a pompous ass.* She raised one arm and summoned a few blades, ready to take advantage of the first opening that presented itself.

A minute passed without any sounds, prompting Serennia to sidle closer to the foot of the bed. She launched herself across the floor, firing the blades in the direction the bolt had come from. Her attacks hit a bare wall. Lord Muretian was nowhere to be found. She rose to her feet and looked around the room until her eyes came to rest on an open door to her left. A closet?

Inch by inch, she approached. Her heart thundered in her chest, heat rising beneath her skin. She prepared a couple more blades and peeked in, slowly craning her neck to peer around the doorway. All she found were piles of weapons and a bare armour stand.

The faint rustle of chain mail was her only warning. She dove to the ground as a sword swung through the air, close enough to nick her cloak as it trailed behind her. Her shoulder slammed against the ground as she fell, sending a jolt of pain up her arm from her fresh injury and dissipating the blades she had conjured. She winced, but tried not to pay it any mind, focusing instead on the armed man that inched closer to her.

Muretian wore his full armour, complete with a small, round shield strapped to the wrist of his off-hand. His sword angled down towards her, poised and ready to strike like a rearing snake with fangs bared. The dim candlelight caught on his polished armour. His lips were twisted into a sneering smile, as if his face was torn between the joy of catching her and the anger at her being in his home. She glared back at him, refusing to show any hint of fear.

"You're not so tough when your opponent fights back, are you?" Muretian taunted. "You'd rather kill me in my sleep and leave, is that it? Don't have what it takes to kill someone who can look you in the eye and watch you do it?" A low laugh rumbled out of his lips before he continued. "If you want to call yourself a killer, at least have the guts to acknowledge what you're doing. Quit hiding behind shadowed knives and unconscious victims."

A quick lunge brought his sword thrusting toward Serennia, forcing her to roll sideways out of the way. Before she could get her bearings, the stab flowed into a wide slash, scoring a cut across her back. She knew she needed to fight back, but the moment she lost the element of surprise he'd gained the upper hand. He was far more experienced than her, forcing her to scramble for an opening. All she needed was a few seconds to conjure a weapon of her own.

"Come on, surely you have more fight in you than that!" His shield smashed down inches from Serennia's ankle. The following upswing caught her jaw with the edge of the shield hard enough to make her vision swim. For a second, everything was out of focus, as if she was seeing the world through a murky window. She could barely register the sword flying towards her neck. She threw herself to the side. If she'd been any slower, she'd have been skewered against the wall.

"Fight me!" Lord Muretian roared. "I'd hoped for a challenge, not some snivelling coward backed into a corner!"

"I'm not here to kill you!" Serennia shouted in response. She wasn't sure why she'd said it. It was an obvious lie, but she hoped it would buy her a few precious seconds.

"You expect me to believe that?" Another slash, another near miss.

"It's the truth! I've been sent to protect you. Like you said, you're an obvious target for whoever killed Lord Tulkarr, and you're too important to Ruddreth to leave unguarded. I was hired to make sure you were safe from the assassin." It was a stupid story, yet somehow doubling down on it felt like her best option.

"I'm not so easily fooled, vagrant. Even if that were the case, I think I've proven that I don't need your protection." He stood his ground, but he didn't go for another attack.

Serennia's whole body ached, her face throbbing from the shield hit. Her vision was still fuzzy at the edges, her sleeve stained red and caked with blood. If she was going to attempt a counter, she would have to be fast and, more importantly, accurate. The moment Lord Muretian even sensed she was trying something, he would finish her.

She held her hands in front of herself, removing her arcane ring with deliberate motions. She set it on the ground, never taking her eyes off Lord Muretian, then backed away until it was out of her reach. One hand came up to wipe some blood off her face. Lord Muretian's eyes darted down to the ring for a brief moment, and Serennia had her opening. A blade blinked into existence beside her fist, which was poised under her ear. She snapped a punch toward Muretian, the sliver of magic following it and continuing on to the nobleman.

He responded with an overhead swing of his sword, aimed at her head, though it came far too late. Before his swing had even reached its halfway point, Serennia's blade sliced through the fingers gripped around his sword. The weapon clattered to the ground, along with most of the fingers on his right hand.

Muretian let out a howl of pain, his uninjured hand rushing to clasp the bloodied stumps where his fingers had been just moments before. When he looked back at her, his eyes were aflame with the sort of fury usually reserved for wild predators. His lips curled back into a snarl, his breaths coming ragged and heavy through clenched teeth.

Serennia smiled in return. She forced herself up from the floor and threw another blade at his neck. Muretian managed to get his shield up in time, the magical weapon driving halfway through before it came to a stop. His shield swung outwards toward her, missing by only a few inches as Serennia leaned back out of the way. She didn't see his foot rising off the ground as the shield passed her, turning into a powerful kick that connected with her stomach.

She stumbled back, her mounting pain stoking her anger and her thirst for victory. She threw two more blades at the man, one aimed at his face, which he blocked with his shield, and another just after that sliced deep across his side. The successful hit caused him to flinch, providing Serennia a chance to fire a shot at his leg. Another magical weapon found the gap in his leg armour and tore through his knee, causing the man's leg to buckle beneath him.

"Is this what you wanted?" It was Serennia's turn to taunt. "You wanted a fight, didn't you? You should be happy. I'm granting your wish."

She moved closer, bringing her right arm into a punch, hoping to goad him into another wild swing with his shield. As she stepped around the anticipated attack, she summoned two more knives around her left arm instead of her right and shot them through the shoulder and elbow of his shield arm. The limb dropped limp to his side, blood pouring out to mar his perfectly maintained armour.

A kick to Muretian's chest knocked him onto his back. Serennia stood over him, arcane energy condensing into a series of daggers over her shoulders. A mask of fear replaced his furious face, his wide eyes reflecting the opalescent daggers pointed at him.

"W-what are you?" he stammered, any sense of bravery or strength now gone.

Six blades plunged into Muretian's chest. His final breaths sputtered out of his lungs, a pool of blood spreading out underneath him with each shallow heave of his chest. Serennia let out a held breath, picked up her ring, took a moment to get her nerves under control, and walked out the way she'd come.

Chapter 14

The line between afternoon and evening blurred as Serennia walked the wide road that connected the outer and inner cities. She held a ball of fried dough in one hand, which she took idle bites from as she strolled through Ruddreth. The food was tasty, though it was mostly a distraction to keep her from thinking about the events at Lord Muretian's manor the previous week.

She arrived at the smithy, a long squat building with unremarkable features nestled between the two sections of the city. Smoke billowed out of a chimney in the back and heat ebbed out of the door like a wave. A steady, rhythmic hammering broke through the din with the piercing notes of metal on metal. A broad man stood next to the anvil, working on some project Serennia couldn't identify. It was little more than a chunk of red-hot metal, slowly thinning and lengthening with each strike.

"Morning, Goril," Serennia called out, loud enough to be heard over the sounds of him working.

The man returned the iron to the furnace and wiped his brow with the back of his hand. His skin was red from the heat, his smock stained with years of soot and burns. Serennia had found his name on the list of papers from the Broken Rose. There were several blacksmiths listed, but only a couple in Ruddreth, and he had been listed with "Trusted" beside his name.

"I was wondering when you'd come back. I don't like keeping this stuff around any longer than I have to. It's too risky." He retrieved a bulging bag from behind the furnace and dropped it at her feet. The contents clattered against each other as the bag sagged on the ground. Goril looked both ways before he spoke again. "I'm all for helping friends of the Rose however I can, but I'd rather do so in ways that won't lead to my death if I'm caught."

"I understand, and I'm sorry for putting you in such a position. I promise I won't ask anything like this of you again." Serennia fished a handful of coins out of the purse that hung from her waist. "Here's the rest. Thank you again for your hard work and discretion."

Goril responded with a nod, pocketing the coins before returning to his work. Serennia hefted the bag over her shoulder and left the smithy, taking the alleyways across the city rather than risk attention on busier streets. After a brief stop to drop the armour off in her room at the Albatross, she went back out to grab a meal at the charity kitchen.

Upon arrival, she found the doors closed with a line forming outside. She recognized many of the regulars, and many of the others certainly fit the look of their clientele. Serennia gave an experimental tug on one of the doors, the locks holding it fast.

"Don't you think we've tried that?" the man beside her sneered. "It's the new rules. Place is only open for dinner now. Can't see how we're supposed to survive on one meal a day." He was met with a chorus of grumbles from the people standing close enough to overhear.

As if on cue, Ralsin flung open the doors before Serennia could voice her questions to the man. She looked at Ralsin, who met her eyes with a solemnity in his own. "I'll explain after everyone's served."

Serennia went inside and took a seat at the table closest to the counter, watching and waiting while the city's destitute came to get what might be their only meal of the day. The volunteers worked with haste, eager to get through the line as quickly as they could manage. The stew smelled delicious as always, yet somehow her appetite had quietened over the course of the last few minutes,

When all the patrons had been served, Ralsin gestured for Serennia. She obliged and he led her into the back room. She wondered if he would bring her to the underground room from before, but it seemed the storeroom was as far as they would go this time.

"I imagine you have some questions about our new rules."

"I thought the whole point of this place was to keep the less fortunate from starving on the streets. To provide a warm meal to anyone who might need it, any time they need it."

"It was, and I wish it could still be. But without the funding from Rosewine, we can't operate like that anymore. We can't afford to offer multiple meals a day, not if we want to have enough to satisfy the crowds. We've decided that our best option is to make a big dinner so that everyone can at least have one meal rather than the fastest handful getting a little while the others get nothing."

"Can't you get funding from somewhere else?" Serennia had a hard time believing none of the nobles in and around Ruddreth were willing to come forward with donations.

"The Ruddran elite look at the people of the outer city as a plague. None of them are willing to sacrifice their own money for anything that might support the poor. Believe me, we've tried. We still have a few kind supporters, but our funds are a fraction of what they were."

A fire was stoked in Serennia's chest, one she hadn't felt for some time. Her hatred of Crennel Brathis, which had been growing dormant in her time away, made itself known once more. How many people would go hungry now because he wouldn't loosen his purse strings? She had always known he was a deplorable man, yet despite the abuses she'd suffered at his hands, this felt like a new low.

"I'm sorry things have come to this. I hope you find a way to get things back to normal soon."

Ralsin nodded, his voice quiet when it came. "Me too, Serennia. Me too."

* * * * *

Serennia practically ran down the stairs to the Nest. By the time she reached the bottom, the noise of her heavy footsteps had drawn the attention of every Sparrow present. She ignored their stares as she bounded across the room, right up to the door that led to Genn's office. Taza stood guard outside as usual.

"Let me in." She didn't bother pleading. He was just as likely to respond to a command as he was to begging, so why waste time?

"Nobody gets in without the boss's explicit invitation."

"Then tell him I need to speak with him." She spoke louder, hoping Genn would hear her through the closed door. "Go on, I'll wait," she added when Taza didn't move.

With a scoff and a roll of his eyes, Taza opened the door just enough for him to squeeze through the opening, then shut it behind him. Serennia heard the lock click into place a moment later, followed by muffled voices from the room beyond. But she was in no mood to wait on their whims. A spike of magic was more than enough to cut through the lock, leaving her free to push open the door.

Judging by Taza's startled expression, he had expected her to wait patiently outside until they were done. He was halfway to the door when she strode through, no doubt planning to slam it closed. Genn, on the other hand, sat behind his desk with the same placid look on his face as always. As if he had been expecting her to be impatient.

Taza opened his mouth, only to be cut off by Genn. "Leave us, Taza. It seems Serennia and I need to have a word in private."

Taza hesitated for the briefest of moments. He glared at Serennia with a blended look of contempt and pride. Then he was gone, the door closing behind him. Serennia took the vacant seat without waiting for it to be offered. Genn watched her with a slight smile. "To what do I owe this pleasure?"

"I need you to tell me more about the Church of Balance."

"What is it you want to know?"

"How do they manage to view evil deeds in a positive light?"

Genn was silent for a time before answering. "That is one of the great misconceptions about the Church of Balance. Many people believe that since they do not punish sins outright, they must view those sins as being moral or just. I assure you, that is not the case. They simply choose to base the punishment on the reasoning rather than the action instead of condemning all who commit even minor sins to a life of failure as the Pentad does.

"The Church of Balance understands that humans are flawed beings. We all fail. Anyone who tells you otherwise is either a liar or a fool. So we must not judge each other for minor misdeeds if those actions were taken to the benefit of someone else."

Serennia nodded, trying to let the information sink into her core. She held on to every word, gripping it tight like a person at sea clinging to a piece of driftwood. "So killing Lord Muretian was good because it saved or otherwise improved the lives of many people at the cost of only one?"

"Precisely. You meted out the justice that his victims deserved. Where the Pentad would have been content to let him face punishment in the afterlife, you prevented him from worsening countless more lives in the here and now."

Serennia had mostly accepted that she had done the right thing in killing Lord Muretian, but it was still good to hear confirmation from someone else. "So let's say there are people starving because their Lord is withholding their food and keeping it all for himself. I know that killing the Lord would allow the food to be redistributed to the people that need it."

Genn reached into one of the drawers of his desk and retrieved a scale, which he set up between them. Serennia wondered if he kept it solely for demonstrations like this one. He set a single coin on one side, then piled the other side with several coins, causing the heavier side to drop as far as the mechanism would allow.

"On one side," he began, gesturing to the single coin, "we have the life of the nobleman, keeping the food for himself because he feels he deserves it. And on the other, we have the lives of the people that will starve to death under his regime. Which side would you pick?"

Serennia was finding that she knew the answer to that, though she wished she didn't. She pointed to the heavier side of the scale, her words evading her.

"A single life is a minor price to pay for several. While few within the Church of Balance would ever resort to murder, I feel their teachings can apply to that just as well as a thief stealing to feed his children. If we accept that the Pentad are flawed, then we must also accept that their form of justice is equally so."

The Pentad *was* flawed. The Arcanaeum operated under their laws, and they were the ones who had killed Serennia's parents. How could beings so purportedly benevolent create orphans? She was done trying to follow their tenets. Everything Genn had told her about the Church of Balance had felt right. It was as though the world made sense for the first time in her life.

"I have to leave Ruddreth," Serennia said. "I have something I need to do. I don't know if I'll be back."

"You are a Sparrow, Serennia. You have always had the freedom to fly anywhere you feel you must. Just know that the Nest will always welcome you home." He smiled at her, one of the first genuine emotions she'd ever seen from the man.

"Thank you, Genn. You've been a bigger help than you can ever know."

Chapter 15

Being back in Alcress was a strange feeling. Part of it felt like coming home, as though Serennia had been on an extended vacation that had come to a bittersweet end. On the other hand, the orderly blocks and squat buildings gave off a feeling of imprisonment from the moment she arrived.

Serennia's eyes had been locked onto Rosewine since she'd first crossed the threshold of the town. The estate loomed in the distance, twice as tall as the surrounding buildings and several times wider. When Hauber had inhabited the place, it had seemed like a beacon of protection for the people of Alcress. In the years since Crennel had taken over, it had warped into an oppressive presence. Guards walked the perimeter or stood atop the roof, threatening harm to anyone unexpected who came too close.

She was more than prepared for that. As she approached, the guards turned towards her. For a moment, they faced her with spears levelled until they got a proper look. Then their eyes widened and their weapons dropped. A few even turned away. Her armour was working exactly as intended.

Most people knew better than to pick a fight with the Undying. Doing so was suicide more often than not, especially for those without any magic. Ragtag militiamen like Crennel had employed wouldn't stand a chance, and it showed as most of them pretended they hadn't seen her.

She wore a hooded cloak to conceal her lack of a mask, as she hadn't wanted to contend with whatever malicious force it contained, but the rest of the armour she wore proudly. Goril had done a fantastic job adapting the plates to her size; it was like the armour had been made for her. She had eschewed a couple of the pieces, forgoing some of the intermediary parts in favour of mobility.

It was nice to be the one causing fear at Rosewine for a change instead of the one afraid.

Serennia threw open the doors and strode into the foyer, drawing the attention of a few of the serving staff, who turned to see who the new arrival was. When they got a good look at her armour, they ran in various directions. She walked through unhindered, leaving the doors open behind her.

It was late enough that Crennel likely would have retired for the night, so she headed straight towards his bedchamber. It was on the other side of the manor, which unfortunately gave him plenty of time to escape should he learn of her presence. She hoped none of his thugs had given away her arrival.

The hallways felt smaller. She hadn't grown that much she was certain, but something had changed. She was done skulking and hiding. For the first time since Lord Hauber's death, she navigated the halls like she belonged there. Rosewine was her home, and it was long past time for her to take it back.

The doors to the master bedroom were the tallest ones in the manor. Lord Hauber had disliked how grandiose they felt and had often mused about having them replaced. They sat at the end of a long hall, wide enough that they barely left any room for the wall. While they were free of any carvings, all the metal parts were plated in gold, half-worn from years of use.

Two guards stood on either side of the doors, their chatting interrupted by the figure striding down the hall. Their stares became apprehensive at once, looking back and forth from each other to her, their spears held halfway at the ready. Serennia continued forward without pause. When she was only a few steps away, the guards pushed the doors open with a silent nod in her direction.

With one last deep breath, quiet enough that she hoped the guards couldn't hear, she walked through the doorway. Crennel's four-poster bed sat against the wall straight ahead, done up with silk sheets and down pillows. Tapestries hung between the windows, which looked out at the mountains to the east, their peaks slicing through the passing clouds. Among the useless frivolities, Crennel was nowhere to be found.

Now what? She couldn't exactly go stomping around the whole damn estate looking for him. *No choice but to wait for the bastard.* Serennia closed the heavy doors behind her and tried to figure out her next move. Crennel's desk sat beneath one of the picture windows, the only thing in the room that hadn't been cleaned to immaculate perfection.

Serennia sat down and scanned the workspace, hoping for anything that might incriminate the man. An inkpot sat in one corner next to an array of pens and a pot of sand opposite a box of wax sticks that were positioned in front of a small melter. Papers littered the space between, mostly letters written in different hands, broken up by half finished responses. As she sifted through the pages, looking at the names scrawled across the bottom, one caught her eye. She removed it from the pile and began to read.

Crennel,

I had hoped taking over my brother's estate might force you to grow up, but it appears I didn't do a good enough job of beating proper sense into you. If only you'd been born a daughter. At least then I could have married you off and rid the family name of your stain. Though considering your wife couldn't tolerate you for more than a couple of years, I doubt even that would have solved my problem.

Did you know that your son has assumed the name of his new father? Given his age, I'd be surprised if he grows up knowing his true parentage.

All this is to say that you are officially disowned. I'm sure you'll continue to use my name like the parasite that you are, but I shall regard you the same as a very distant cousin at best. Do not bother writing back.

-Vantine Brathis

Must be something in the Brathis blood that makes them insufferable. It's a wonder Lord Hauber escaped it. If his outward appearance was to be believed, of course. *No.* She wasn't going down that road again. She was here for one reason only.

Serennia busied herself reading through more of the letters, though none of them were anywhere near as interesting as the first. Several of the unfinished ones were responses from Crennel to his father, some of them begging for forgiveness, while others were furious rebukes penned in a far messier script.

As she neared the end of the stack, the sound of door handles being turned broke the silence. Serennia rose from the chair, allowing herself a long inhale before the door opened. Crennel entered in a hurry, pausing only to slam the doors shut behind him, then turned to face her.

"I told you to send notice before coming here. How many of my staff saw you? I'd like to know how many rumours I'll need to quash because of your ignorance." Crennel steadied himself, holding one shaky hand out as if to forestall her response. "No matter. I assume your presence here means you've found her?"

He looked thinner than Serennia remembered, like his skin had been stretched across his bones. His cheeks were sunken, his eyes dim almost to the point of lifelessness.

Was this really the villain who had plagued her mind? This emaciated, piteous man who couldn't even stand without trembling? It had to be an act. There was no way it wasn't.

Serennia lowered her hood with methodical slowness. Crennel's eyes widened until she thought they would fall out, his hopeful grin fading into a tight line. Oh, how she wished she could have captured that look on his face. She made sure to savour it.

To his credit, he played off the brief shock well, his face snapping back to a more neutral expression. "Look who's come crawling back. Where'd you get that ridiculous armour from? You don't actually expect me to believe you joined the Undying in such a short time, do you?"

"I took it from the corpse of the man you sent after me." It was blunt, but effective. Her words were enough to arrest whatever had been about to leave Crennel's mouth. "You've been a drain on this world long enough, Crennel."

The skeletal man tried to put on a brave face, though the sweat along his brow belied his fear. "I am an asset to this world. You are nothing but a snivelling child who spent too long freeloading off my uncle's achievements."

Serennia's rage burned hotter with each word out of his mouth. She took a step forward and relished in the way he flinched back. "Yet you're the one who had to take his anger out on a young girl. Did it feel good, the sense of superiority you felt from attacking a child, you pathetic worm?"

A blade appeared above Serennia's shoulder and shot forwards. The attack sliced across Crennel's arm before he had time to react. Blood welled up from the cut, seeping into the sleeve of his shirt. He clasped a frail hand to the wound, his other hand extending towards her. The arcane ring on his finger began to glow, a thumbnail-sized orb of energy materializing in front of him. His eyes fixed on her. Serennia waited until the ball was almost fully formed before she fired another blade at his hand.

An anguished scream erupted from Crennel's lungs as his attack fizzled into the air. He released his arm to clutch where his two smallest fingers had been, though it did little to stem the flow of blood. His breaths came in heavy seethes through gritted teeth, his fingers limp on the ground, one of them still wearing the ring.

"Please! Have mercy! I'm sorry!" His apologies sounded like a desperate child trying to avoid trouble.

"You're sorry? You're *sorry*?" Serennia's voice continued to rise as she launched another blade that opened Crennel's thigh. "You spent years making my life miserable. You tried to kill me in a fit of rage, and now you think you can just apologize and it will go away?"

Several more blades appeared in the air around her, all poised to launch into Crennel at a moment's notice. With each new weapon that blinked into existence, his eyes grew wider. Her fists clenched at her sides, the heat of her anger drowning out the discomfort of her magic. She refused to use the ring for this. This one was personal.

A blade launched forward and cut across the side of Crennel's chest, followed by another that scraped his opposite shoulder. One more pierced through his foot and into the floor. Crennel yelled for his guards, which brought a storm of footsteps up the hall. The armed men threw open the doors, then caught a glimpse of Serennia and froze.

"What are you waiting for? Kill her!"

Serennia turned her gaze to the guards assembled at the entry. She kept most of her weapons trained on Crennel, but a few of them rotated to face the new arrivals. "What's wrong? I believe you were given orders."

For a moment the guards looked between themselves, spears held still in hesitant hands. A couple of them gave Serennia an appraising look from head to toe, like they were scanning for weak points or sizing up their odds. After a minute, they retreated back down the hallway.

"Looks like their purchased loyalty only goes so far," Serennia said as Crennel yelled after his fleeing reinforcements.

"Please. I'll do anything. I'll pay you. I'll buy you your own estate far away from here. Whatever you want. Just please don't kill me." Tears began to form in the corners of Crennel's eyes.

"There's nothing I want from you." Another attack sliced his knee and he dropped to the ground. His clothes were more bloodstained than not, his face covered in tears and sweat, one hand still holding in the other. He fought up to a kneeling position, hands in front of his chest. "Please. Forgive me. You don't have to do this."

A firm kick to the centre of his chest sent Crennel sprawling onto his back. "I know damn well that I don't have to do this. But you have no idea how much I *want* to."

Serennia raised one arm into the air, and the blades around her quivered in place. Every point turned to converge on Crennel, a dozen slivers of opalescent light lingering above him like an executioner's axe, waiting for the sentence to fall. He didn't bother trying to get up anymore. His blood stained the carpet, while mutters of "Please" and "I'm sorry" left his mouth in a steady stream. She hesitated.

Was this really how she wanted it all to end? By carving up a whimpering man who couldn't defend himself? He was a monster that had ruined her life. A monster who had abused her to feel better. A monster whose father hated him, and whose son would never even know he existed. Her mind flashed back to her last night at Rosewine. Would Crennel have shown her mercy?

Her teeth clenched so hard her jaw hurt. Why couldn't this be easy? *Think of the starving people outside the charity kitchen. Their lives depend on his death.* Did they though? She had little doubt that if she demanded Crennel to fund the kitchen in exchange for his life, he'd do it.

She remembered Genn's teachings, pictured the Cosmic Scale in her head, tried to picture Crennel being outweighed by the lives she would save.

Damn Crennel. Damn him and everything he'd done to her. How dare he be so horrible only to turn into a pathetic waste of a man when she could finally get revenge? The world would be better off without him. It had to be.

Just as she was about to finish him off, a voice from the doorway stopped her.

"Serennia, enough. You are not a butcher."

She turned to see Laerine with her hands held before her, grey hair tucked into its usual tight bun. Her face portrayed no obvious emotion, only recognition of everything happening mere steps from her. Serennia wondered what Laerine thought about the scene, whether the woman approved of her actions. She searched her eyes for any hint to no avail.

With a sigh, Serennia let her suspended blades fade. She held a hand towards Crennel. Relief flooded across his face, his eyes lighting with gratitude, and he reached forward to accept her offer. Just as his hand was about to reach hers, she fired a single blade, piercing straight through his chest. His eyes froze in shock as his body crumpled, the life already gone from his corpse.

Serennia looked into Crennel's lifeless eyes and felt nothing.

Epilogue

Serennia sat in the gardens of the estate, still wearing her adapted Undying armour. A gentle wind blew, rustling the leaves of the trees that ran around the outside, forming a makeshift perimeter housing the flowers and shrubs. This area had been her training grounds. Hauber had set up various targets for her to aim at, some of them half hidden behind foliage and branches.

"We should talk about your future, Serennia." Laerine's voice sounded behind her. Serennia wasn't sure how long the woman had been standing there. "Rosewine is currently without a proper heir, and I can think of nobody better than Lord Hauber's daughter."

"I'm not his daughter. I'm not sure I ever was."

"Surely you don't believe that. Lord Hauber loved you like you were his own."

Serennia let out a resigned sigh. "Either way, I have no interest in taking over Rosewine."

"But if you don't, then Rosewine could be forced to close."

She couldn't let that happen. That would defeat the whole purpose of coming back to Rosewine. Laerine had never been anything but kind to Serennia. She deserved more.

"You can run it. You've served three generations of Brathis Lords. I'm sure you know the details by now."

Laerine pursed her lips, her eyes drifting to the mountains that rose in the distance. When she spoke, it almost seemed more to herself than to Serennia. "It wouldn't be right. This is the Brathises' legacy, and it should go to you. Not me."

"Fine, I'll take the role. And as my first act as head of the household, I pass the title and all it entails to you." Serennia smirked.

"You always were a sneaky little thing, weren't you?" Laerine laughed. "Why do you so fervently refuse such a tremendous gift? Are you sure this is what you want?"

"This house is a painful memory for me. As much as I loved my time with Lord Hauber, a part of me can't stop wondering if he trained me for his own gains. If I take over Rosewine then I'm accepting the life Lord Hauber planned for me. And I don't know if I want that."

"If you're certain this is what you want, then I won't force it on you. But if you'd like to come home, you can have the master bedroom. I'm more than content in the room I've had since I started here."

"No, Laerine. I'm sorry, but this place isn't my home anymore."

Laerine nodded, seeming to understand. Serennia wondered what Laerine would think of her if she knew what she'd become. Sure, she'd seen her kill Crennel. But did Laerine suspect the extent of it? Did she know the depths of what Serennia had become? Or did she assume this had been a one-time incident, fuelled by rage and a thirst for revenge?

"Then I suppose everything is settled." Laerine helped Serennia to her feet and wrapped her in a hug, which she returned with enthusiasm. When they pulled apart, Laerine reached into her pocket and produced a signet ring. "At least take this with you. Let it serve as a reminder that Rosewine will always be here for you."

"Thank you." Serennia slipped the ring onto one of her fingers. It was heavier than she'd expected, the Rosewine logo embossed on the flat top.

"Enjoy your new life, Serennia. You've earned it."

"I sure have, haven't I?" Serennia joked. She hoped Laerine didn't notice the quiver in her voice.

www.ingramcontent.com/pod-product-compliance
Lightning Source LLC
Jackson TN
JSHW081220070925
90477JS00003B/5
* 9 7 8 1 0 6 9 5 5 2 4 0 2 *